PRAISE FOR TED DEKKER'S
BOOKS OF HISTORY CHRONICLES

"Young and old alike will enjoy this latest offering. Dekker fans will love this new story from the Circle universe and new readers will undoubtedly be sucked in to the greatness that is Ted Dekker. [*Chosen*] is a superb beginning to what is sure to be a fantastic series."

—*Bookshelf Reviews*

"Toss away all your expectations, because *Showdown* is one of the most original, most thoughtful, and most gripping reads I've been through in ages . . . Breaking all established story patterns or plot formulas, you'll find yourself repeatedly feeling that there's no way of predicting what will happen next . . . The pacing is dead-on, the flow is tight, and the epic story is down-right sneaky in how it unfolds. Dekker excels at crafting stories that are hard to put down, and *Showdown* is the hardest yet."

—*Infuze Magazine*

"As a producer of movies filled with incredible worlds and heroic characters, I have high standards for the fiction I read. Ted Dekker's novels deliver big with mind-blowing, plot-twisting page turners. Fair warning—this trilogy will draw you in at a breakneck pace and never let up. Cancel all plans before you start because you won't be able to stop once you enter *Black*."

—Ralph Winter, Producer of *X-Men, X2: X-Men United,*
and *Planet of the Apes*

"[In *Showdown*] Dekker delivers his signature exploration of good and evil in the context of a genuine thriller that could further enlarge his already sizable audience."

—*Publishers Weekly*

You've heard about the critical raves,
but here's what readers are saying online about

The Books of History Chronicles

(Black, Red, White, Showdown, and Saint)

This trilogy is a MUST READ! Suspenseful, insightful, fast-paced, and certainly life-impacting. Ted Dekker is a master of bringing Truth close to home, in a way that causes us the readers to see and feel it in a fresh way.

D. (Pittsburgh, PA)

Whew, ok I've read all three books in the Circle Trilogy back to back and all I can say is man what a ride. Ted Dekker has to be one of our generations great story tellers, this story of Thomas Hunter's fight to save mankind from a terrible virus intended to destroy the world is sure to become a Christian fiction classic much like Lewis's "Narnia" Series and Frank Perretti's "This Present Darkness".

Todd (Mount Vernon, WA)

This was the first book by Ted Dekker that I've ever read. It was all I needed to be hooked for life! Ted Dekker has a way with words and storytelling that not many authors have anymore. He draws you in and you have to make yourself stop for daily functions such as eating and occasional breathing!

J. (South Carolina)

I cannot say enough good things about this book and series. It can change how you think. If a book can do that it is an amazing thing. I recommend it without reservation. The Circle Trilogy was my first Ted Dekker book, but it will not be the last.

Teresa (Parkersburg, WV)

Fascinating. . . worth the read. . . . I enjoyed the series so much I bought a second set as a gift even before I finished White.

Slwaldaias (Yerington, NV)

*This book, like Red, picks up where the last left off. The book is very quickly paced and makes it easy to fly through even if you're trying to slowly read it to take everything in. **By the time you're finished reading, you're just left speechless** with all the twists and turns in the plot. These three books are the best I've read in quite a while.*

Becky (Mentor, OH)

***This is an incredible book!** Like all of Dekkers masterpieces, this plays with your emotions until your drained! By the end of a Dekker book, you are challenged to think, and on the brink of doing a million push-ups, (or crying depending on who you are.) Read this great book!*

Media Lover

*The writing is superb; fast paced, and always leaves the reader on the edge of the seat. **Ted Dekker is a writer of rare creativity and imagination.***

Michael

*As a consummate reader of fiction I can honestly say that this trilogy penned by Mr. Dekker is **perhaps the most absorbing and well executed tales I have ever read.***

Barb

***These books were simply amazing.** I first heard about it after reading Thr3e. Once I picked it up, I could not set it down.*

J. (Seaside, CA)

*This guy is truly amazing. He's written straight novels, romance thrillers, psychological suspense, and now a fantasy thriller. He stretches and stretches, yet never becomes distorted, uneven, or sloppy. **I suspect that a generation from*** now, Dekker's writings will be essential reading for those who wish to study spiritually motivated literature.

Tommy (Federal Way, WA)

Absolutely a terrific trilogy! I got the first book, "Black" from the library, and when I finished it and realized it was a trilogy, ordered all three books the same day . . .next day! Incredible book full of drama, mystery, and beautiful love stories . . . both for people and God. You won't regret reading them . . .

June (Florida)

This may be one of my top 5 books of all time. The whole thing was engaging and outstanding. There was no lull anywhere. Each page and each chapter had interesting things happening. I've since read other's of Ted's including Red, White, Heaven's Wager, and Three. All awesome.

Sgun73 (Carmel, IN)

*This is the first of a trilogy—but don't be intimidated by the fact that you must read three books to journey through all of Dekker's tale. **This is an incredible fantasy, written with such a furious pace that it is hard to put down.** I was wise enough to not start any of the three books until I had all of them—unfortunately for my wife I did have all of them when I started reading them, and I just went from one to the next to the final one. Incredible!*

Zachary (Wake Forest, NC)

***I am addicted to great story telling. Ted Dekker is now my main drug dealer.** I'm halfway through Red, the second book of the Circle Trilogy, and have now put Mr. Dekker in my pantheon with Robert Jordan, Stephen Lawhead, C. S. Lewis and Professor Tolkien. This guy writes literary heroine.*

Mike (Centreville, Alabama)

*I like books with lots of action. Dekker delivers. I love books that make you expand your inner universe. Dekker delivers. I enjoy books with great romance. Dekker delivers. I enjoy exotic locales. Dekker delivers. **I LOVE this book!** I highly recommend reading it! It totally keeps you on the edge of your seat from the very second you start until it leaves on a cliff-hanger for the next book in the series. You gotta get it!*

Trinedy

*The Circle Trilogy—Black, and the subsequent Red and White—is not the sort of book I usually read but I was persuaded to try it by a friend who had read it and loved it. I thought I would listen to just enough to be able to say I tried but couldn't get into it —**Boy was I wrong!***

Lynne (Montgomery, AL)

***These books touched me more than any other books I have ever read.** I was reluctant to buy the books when I first heard what they were about. Finally said, "what the heck" and purchased them based on the great reviews. I am so happy I did. They are unlike any other books I have ever read and really cannot compare them to anything.*

Rich L (Pennsylvania)

***Quite possibly this is one of the most incredible books ever written.** Definitely that I've read. Too bad I can't give it more than just five stars! I was so in awe of this story. I can't recall the last time I read a novel with such depth and magnitude.*

Sir iliad (Pennsylvania)

***This is one book you can not put down.** I read all three books in three days. If you want a book to keep you occupied, then read this book.*

Cheri

*I just finished Red, and all I can say is "Wow"! This story just keeps getting better. Is Ted Dekker talented or what? Before I became a Chritian, I used to read secular suspense. **I must say this is better than anything I've read not only in Christian writing, but in fiction period.***

Nicholas (Salt Lake City, UT)

*WOW! **Ted Dekker continued to blow my socks off** in book two of the trilogy Black, Red, and White. The book held my interest, in fact it drew me to continually read to the point that I finished it way faster than most books that I have read (I think my wife was ready to put me out with the dog).*

William (Stouffville, Ontario, Canada)

*I am new to Ted Dekker: but I'll be getting further acquainted. The story kept me turning the pages; some of my guesses were prescient and others missed the mark. Captivating! **Where have I been as this author emerged in contemporary mystery fiction?** A great read!*

Lori (Lake Forest, CA)

*It is unbelievable how Ted can take your mind in so many directions at once and then tie all of it together and really put a spiritual meaning to the whole thing. **This is one of my favorite books of all time.***

Franklin (Warner Robins, GA)

*Ted Dekker did it again. **He got me wrapped around his fingers** (or writing I suppose). After months of wait I was not disappointed. This book is one of his best yet.*

Rafa S.

Dekker pulls out all the stops in this tale. I don't want to give too much away, but he really grabs you by the pants and doesn't let go! The blurbs are right, this ranks right up there with King and Koontz, not to be missed!

Matt (Mendocino, CA)

CHAOS

teddekker.com

DEKKER FANTASY

BOOKS OF HISTORY CHRONICLES

THE LOST BOOKS
Chosen
Infidel
Renegade
Chaos

THE CIRCLE TRILOGY
Black
Red
White

THE PARADISE BOOKS
Showdown
Saint
Sinner (SEPTEMBER 2008)

Skin
House (with Frank Peretti)

DEKKER MYSTERY

Kiss (JANUARY 2009)
Blink of an Eye

MARTYR'S SONG SERIES
Heaven's Wager
When Heaven Weeps
Thunder of Heaven
The Martyr's Song

THE CALEB BOOKS
Blessed Child
A Man Called Blessed

DEKKER THRILLER

THR3E
Obsessed
Adam

CHAOS

A LOST BOOK

TED DEKKER

THOMAS NELSON
Since 1798

NASHVILLE DALLAS MEXICO CITY RIO DE JANEIRO BEIJING

Published in Nashville, Tennessee, by Thomas Nelson. Thomas Nelson is a registered trademark of Thomas Nelson, Inc.

Published in association with Thomas Nelson and Creative Trust, Inc., 5141 Virginia Way, suite 320, Brentwood, TN 37027.

Thomas Nelson books may be purchased in bulk for educational, business, fund-raising, or sales promotional use. For information, please e-mail SpecialMarkets@ThomasNelson.com.

Publisher's Note: This novel is a work of fiction. Names, characters, places, and incidents are either products of the author's imagination or used fictitiously. All characters are fictional, and any similarity to people living or dead is purely coincidental.

Page Design by Casey Hooper
Map Design by Chris Ward

Library of Congress Cataloging-in-Publication Data

Dekker, Ted, 1962–
   Chaos / Ted Dekker.
       p. cm. — (The lost books ; bk. 4)
   Summary: The four heroic young Forest Guard recruits embark on their last mission to recover the lost Books of History before the Dark One unleashes their power to enslave humanity.
   ISBN 978-1-59554-372-1 (hardcover)
   [1. Fantasy. 2. Christian life—Fiction.] I. Title.
   PZ7.D3684Ch 2008
   [Fic]—dc22

                                                                                                                2008002896

Printed in the United States of America

09 10 11 QW 10 9 8

beginnings

O our story begins in a world totally like our own, yet completely different. What once happened seems to be repeating itself thousands of years later.

But this time the future belongs to the young, to the warriors, to the lovers. To those who can follow hidden clues and find a great treasure which will unlock the mysteries of life and wealth.

Thirteen years have passed since the lush, Colored Forests were turned into desert by Teeleh, enemy of Elyon and vilest of all creatures. Evil now rules the land and shows itself as a painful, scaly disease that covers the flesh of the Horde living in the wasteland.

The powerful green waters, once precious to Elyon, with the exception of seven small lakes surrounded by seven small forests, have vanished from the earth. Those few who have chosen to follow the ways of Elyon are now called Forest Dwellers, bathing once daily in the powerful waters to cleanse their skin of the disease.

The number of their sworn enemy, the Horde, has grown, and the Forest Guard has been severely diminished by war, forcing Thomas, supreme commander, to lower the army's recruitment age to sixteen. A thousand young recruits have shown themselves worthy and now serve in the Forest Guard.

From among the thousand, four young fighters—Johnis, Silvie, Billos, and Darsal—have been handpicked by Thomas to lead.

Unbeknownst to Thomas and those in the forests, our four heroes have also been chosen by the legendary white Roush, guardians of all that is good, for a far greater mission, and they are forbidden to tell a soul.

Their quest is to find the seven original Books of History, which together hold the power to destroy humankind. They were given the one book in the Roush's possession and have recovered three more. They must now find the other three books before the Dark One finds them and unleashes their power to enslave humanity.

Although the full extent of the power contained in these sealed books is unknown, the four have discovered a few disturbing facts about them: They have discovered that only *four* of the seven books exist in their own reality; the other three are on Earth, made invisible until the day when all seven are united. They have discovered that they can cross to Earth using four of the books together. And they have discovered that the Dark One who seeks the seven books to enslave humanity is not in their reality but on Earth.

In keeping with their mission, Johnis and his companions have used the four books to travel to Earth, where they must now find the final three books before the Dark One does.

But Earth is not a nice place to go looking for books.

one

Johnis and Silvie stood on the cliff, silenced by the sheer size of the hazy valley before them.

A sea of towering buildings, gray at this distance, had been built between ribbons of flat rock that crawled with horseless buggies. The city was constructed of structures that looked to be as large as all of Middle Forest under one roof. The entire Horde city looked like a village by comparison.

"It's called 'Las Vegas,' you say?" Johnis asked.

"That's what the sign by the road said," Silvie responded, her voice high-strung. "What do you think?"

"I think I prefer the Horde."

"It is the Horde! They've conquered the world and turned it into rock."

"You know this?" he asked, astonished. "I thought Thomas

went into the Histories, not the future. This looks more advanced than any Histories I could imagine."

Johnis glanced at the two Books of History in his hands. "We're down to our two books. We have to assume that Karas and Darsal made it through with two more. And that the three in this reality are now visible. But how do we find them? They could be scattered anywhere."

"Forget the books for now," Silvie cried. "We have to find Karas and Darsal first."

"Of course," Johnis said, pacing, "but our mission is to find all seven books, and all seven are now in this reality, visible, ready to be found. We have two; Karas and Darsal have two; that leaves the last three—only Elyon knows where—in this cursed place."

"You think Alucard is here?"

She reached for his hand and held it in her own. Not out of affection, but because after hours alone in this unnerving place she needed to be close to someone. To him.

And judging by the slight quiver in his hand, Johnis needed comfort as well.

"I'm afraid, Johnis."

"We made the right choice, Silvie." But his voice was filled with doubt. "We're here to find the seven books before the Dark One does. We'll do that or die trying."

"Spoken like the good old Johnis we all know so well."

"Something's wrong with us," he said, looking at her. "I don't feel like myself."

"Really? You just now noticed?"

Johnis returned his attention to the valley. A dull roar rose from the city. "So . . . where are we?"

"I told you," Silvie said. "We're in hell."

She tilted her head up at the sound of a distant roar. A huge white bird with fixed wings soared through the blue sky.

"Dear Elyon, look at the size of that thing." Johnis grabbed her hand and pulled her toward the boulders. They vaulted over one and came to a stop in the shade of several larger rocks. "I've seen them all day," Silvie said. "We've been spotted by now."

Johnis looked skyward. "They're birds?"

"If the buggies are ants, then maybe those monsters are birds," she said, sliding to her seat. "Either way, they can't possibly be good. If they're the enemy, which we have to assume, they can't be beaten, not by us."

His soft brown eyes searched hers, his mind spinning behind the fine features, messy brown hair, and high cheekbones. If there was one person who would remain strong in the most difficult situation, clinging to principle and all that was right, it was Johnis. He'd proven that over and over again.

"I need you, Johnis. I'm . . . I'm lost. My emotions seem to be getting the better of me."

Johnis removed his eyes from hers and looked about, dazed.

"Maybe this is what happens when you vanish from one reality and reappear in another," she said. "What if all our innards didn't come through right?"

Johnis stood, withdrew his knife, and twirled it once. Then again, twice this time. Silvie was the master with knives, but he performed the maneuver with surprising ease.

"Our bodies seem to have come through in one piece," he said.

Silvie jerked out two of her knives, flipped them into the air in perfect symmetry, caught them by their blades, and flung them at a dead log with a flip of her wrists. They plunged into the wood with scarcely a splinter to separate them.

"You haven't lost your skill," Johnis said. "You've searched these cliffs?" he asked, pointing absently at the mounds of rocks and hills.

"Every last mole hole."

"No sign of Darsal or Karas."

"Or Alucard," she said. "Or Billos."

"Time," he said, facing her.

"Clearly it's not a consistent thing."

He nodded. "I left only moments after you and appeared hours later."

"For all we know, Karas has been here for a month," Silvie said.

"And if we're in the Histories Thomas spoke about, we've gone back in time perhaps thousands of years."

Silvie retrieved her knives and slipped them into sheaths on either thigh. "None of this helps the situation."

"No, but it gives us a starting point."

"Darsal and Karas," Silvie said. If she hadn't spent so much time looking for them already, she might share some of his enthusiasm. "Like I said—"

"We have to get into that city," Johnis interrupted, looking east.

She instantly noticed the boyish look that suddenly brightened his eyes. "Not before we understand what we're getting into."

He jerked his head to face her. "No, now. While we still have a chance of finding Karas and Darsal. Before they end up in captivity . . . or worse."

"What makes you think they went into the city?"

"Where else would they go?"

"We are not going into the city without a plan that makes perfect sense to both of us," Silvie said. "We don't have the third fighting group to sacrifice this time."

It was a low blow, but he let the accusation roll off his back.

"You said you saw one of their roads over the hills?" he demanded, turning south. "How far?"

"A half-hour walk, right over the large knoll. But I don't want to rush off without feeling better about this. Not after last time. Please, we can't just walk down the road in our battle dress, climb to the top of their tallest tower, and scream for Darsal and Karas to come out of hiding."

"I do have a plan," Johnis said, with a slight grin. "Are you with me?"

"What plan?"

"Part of the plan is that you trust me. Are you with me?"

Silvie was surprised by the sudden comfort his confidence brought her. And to be perfectly honest, she did trust him. Almost as much as she loved him.

"Will we live to tell?" she demanded.

"I have no idea."

She paused, then walked past him toward the road, guessing his plan started there. "Something is definitely wrong with us."

"RIGHT OVER THE KNOLL," SILVIE HAD SAID. BUT THE ROAR from the road announced its presence loudly enough.

Johnis hurried up the last part of the hill, bent over in a crouch. Standard battle guards made of leather covered his forearms and his thighs, but he preferred a blue tunic rather than the chest protectors that many of the Forest Guard wore. A month ago this young man had never seen a sword swung in battle. Now his forearm and calf guards were scarred from head-to-head confrontation with Horde.

Seeing him scramble up the knoll ahead of her, Silvie was struck by his transformation in such a short time. His skin was darkened by the desert sun, highlighting cords of muscle in his legs and arms. He might only be sixteen, but he looked much older now—in her mind he was the best of any man she'd met.

She had opted for a dark leather skirt with thigh guards. Her blonde, tangled hair was drawn back to clear her eyes. Wide wristbands broke the line between her well-toned arms and her small hands. "Delicate," Johnis called them once. Never mind that they could wield any weapon with more power and accuracy than his, which weren't large by any unit of measure.

They both wore the same leather boots that had taken them into the Black Forest on two occasions now.

"Slow down," she'd demanded ten minutes earlier.

"I'll slow down when I can make sense of this world," he had said. "We're losing light!" And he had been right; the sun was setting.

"Don't rush into another trap."

That had slowed him some, but now he could hardly control his enthusiasm. He scrambled up the sandy slope that rose above the road and flung himself to his elbows at the top. Silvie dropped in beside him and looked at the road below.

A wide road built of black stone ran over the desert, split by a straight white dash. A building with a large black and red sign marked by the word TEXON stood on this side of the road, and two of the buggies were situated next to what looked like upright feeding troughs.

Having drunk its fill, one of the buggies pulled out onto the road to resume its journey.

"Dear Elyon," Johnis muttered.

Silvie glanced at him and saw that his jaw hung open. His eyes weren't on the feeding station, rather on the road beyond and on the speeding buggies that flew over the road on wheels that looked like they were floating.

"It's magic!" Johnis cried.

"Or worse," Silvie agreed.

"But they aren't animals. They're made out of solid material. I've never seen anything like it!"

"What did I tell you? They look dangerous."

"That's never stopped you before."

He said it without even looking at her, perhaps hardly hearing himself, but the words pulled Silvie into a different world. One in which she would be the first into battle, screaming to avenge her mother's death, urging Johnis to swing his sword.

In this world she was evidently more cautious. She wasn't sure she liked that.

Johnis watched a red buggy approach from their right, then fly past. "It's five, six, maybe seven times faster than a horse at a full gallop. Who in their right mind would walk?"

"We'll kill ourselves."

"It's their land. We do things their way, as we agreed," Johnis said. "If the Horde . . ."

One of the Horde suddenly appeared from a car and walked to a large green garbage receptacle. For the first time, Silvie saw one of history's inhabitants closely enough to make out some detail.

Long golden hair. Blue trousers that hugged the young woman's body. A pink shirt. White moccasins. But it was the woman's face and arms that made Silvie blink as she watched.

There was no trace of disease on her skin, which meant that this particular inhabitant from the Histories was not Horde.

"She's not diseased," Johnis whispered.

They watched her dispose of her garbage and climb into a brown buggy, then speed from the feeding station. Toward the city.

"It's not a Horde city!" Johnis said, pushing himself up in such a way that anyone below would have clearly seen him above the rise, had they been looking.

Silvie grabbed his shoulder and pulled him back down. "That means nothing. They could be the precursors to the Horde, just as evil. Or a different kind of Horde. For all we know, they carry their disease under their skin."

"True. But having the same skin makes blending with them all that much easier. We have to get our hands on a buggy!"

"Our battle dress doesn't blend."

"Then we change!" Johnis faced her, eyes bright. "You could wait here and cover my back. If I'm not successful, we'll try another approach."

"What is your approach?"

He remained silent for a few beats, then jumped to his feet. "Cover my back."

two

Silvie raced along at Johnis's elbow, down the slope and directly toward the feeding station, aware with each step that her nerves were raw beyond reason. She felt more fear than she'd felt facing Teeleh himself.

Still Johnis strode on, as if he'd been here a dozen times.

"You're good, Johnis?" she whispered.

He didn't turn or answer. If it was the air that was affecting them, they would both feel it. So much for simple explanations.

"Johnis? Are you sure this is the best solution?"

He turned and she saw that his face was pale, not by the waning light, but for lack of blood. "I'm good," he said, but his voice trembled.

She took a small amount of comfort from their unity in despair.

He slowed to a walk, pulled his tunic straight, and headed for the stables. The sign bearing the word TEXON stuttered and came to life, glowing red and white and black. Silvie caught her breath and stopped. *Is it a warning?*

She instinctively crouched. "We've been seen!"

Johnis halted, staring up at the sign. Then plowed on.

Silvie hurried to catch him. She took his elbow, wanting to be close. He might find some comfort in showing his bravado, but she had lost her stomach for it. Ice ran through her veins, chilling her in the face of a gently hot desert breeze.

And then they were there, next to the building, with flat gray rock under their feet and a perfectly smooth glass wall before them. They could see plainly into the lighted building, where an attendant surrounded by hundreds of brightly colored boxes and tubes and bags stared back at them.

A stack of folded papers sat just inside the wall. THE LAS VEGAS HERALD. JUNE 7, 2033. Then in huge letters across the top: DROUGHT.

Johnis and Silvie stood immobilized by the wonder of such perfectly formed surroundings. The squareness and roundness of everything was breathtaking. The light was magical.

"He sees us," Silvie said, her voice cracking. "He looks like a warrior!"

Johnis began to move toward a door made of the same glass.

"Johnis, we want the buggy, not him! Don't for a minute assume he's not a throater."

"We can't just take the buggy with him watching," Johnis snapped. "Maybe he'll give it to us."

And then he was pulling the door open and stepping inside the building. Silvie released his arm and followed him past the glass door.

They stood at the entrance, side by side, facing the attendant, who didn't seem too surprised or put off by their presence. He stood taller than they did and was at least twice their weight. His head was bald and a black goatee hung off his thick chin. Tattoos ran up from each elbow and disappeared beneath a light blue shirt, then coiled up the sides of his neck and around the back of his lumpy skull.

This one had seen his share of fights. Silvie's heart pounded, but the fact that this tattooed slugger with blue eyes wasn't reaching for a sword under his counter was only a small relief.

She removed her fingers from the bone-handled knife at her waist when she saw his eyes flitter to it.

"Pardon two wearied travelers," Johnis said in his most polite voice. "We've lost our horses to the desert and need a buggy to finish our journey to the city."

The man just stared. He wore silver earrings in each lobe. No indication that he was a Scab beyond the fact that he looked to be a bit stupid.

"Can you help us?" Silvie asked. "Or are you just going to stare at us?"

She felt Johnis's elbow in her ribs.

"This look like the Excalibur?" the man asked evenly. "We got gas; we got junk food. Buy what you need and take a hike."

Johnis glanced at Silvie. Evidently encouraged by the man's nonsensical response, he stepped in and took on an air of supreme confidence.

"We would fit in at the Excalibur? How is that?"

"You're gladiators, right? So buy what you need and go die somewhere else."

"Our mission is beyond the talk of fools and commoners," Johnis said. "Not that you look like a fool or commoner—far from it."

"You deaf?" The man wasn't interested in whatever Johnis was trying to serve up. Neither was Silvie.

Johnis snatched up a rectangular package marked *Snickers*, ripped it open, and stared at the brown square exposed. He sniffed what looked to be a food bar. "We're quite hungry," he said, then shoved the food into his mouth and bit deeply.

The bald man didn't budge.

Johnis smacked his lips and took another bite. "Oh! That's simply . . . Oh, dear Elyon, this is fantastic!" And by all that Silvie could see, Johnis was truly enraptured with the brown food in his fist. "Try it!" He shoved the bar to her.

Back to the attendant: "You wouldn't happen to know about the Books of History, would you?"

Judging by the man's stone face, he was either a complete imbecile or he was so unprepared for Johnis's arrogance that he had lost track of his thoughts. He was the kind who thought with his fists.

"Johnis, I really think—"

"I thought not. If you hear anyone mention the Books of History, tell them Johnis and Silvie are alive and well and wish to meet with them. In the meantime, we need a buggy. Can you help us?"

Beat.

"What about the red one on the far side of the feeding station? It looked unused to me."

"The Chevy? It's a car, not a buggy." The man's lips twitched into a barely discernible grin. "You have no idea how close you are to a slap upside the head. And I doubt the boss would have a problem with me taking care of a couple of fruits trying to steal his little cherry while he's in LA."

"Perfect! We'll take the cherry Chevy. Have you had a go in it?"

"Look—"

"No, you look, you thick-headed fool! I'm going to throw you a bone here, but you have to go with me. We may look like fruits to you, but there's far more meat between these ears than you are used to. If you play with us, you could walk out of these stables a rich fellow. That doesn't interest you?"

Johnis had lost his mind. Silvie knew what he was trying, but she had no confidence he would succeed. She inched her hands to the blade at her side.

"Now, tell me if you've ridden the Chevy," Johnis said before the man could respond.

"The Chevy—yes."

19

"Good. Then making it go can't require too much intelligence. I'll make you a bet: one gold coin says I can make the Chevy go and leave you standing by your feeding trough before you can stop me."

Johnis pulled out a roughly hewn gold coin from his pocket, one of five he had on him. Thomas had instituted them as one form of currency in the forests after nuggets of the soft colorful metal had been found in the river near Middle and claimed by the Guard. The chosen had each received twenty coins upon their return from the desert with the Catalina cacti.

He flipped the coin through the air. It landed on the counter with a loud clunk, bounced once, and toppled next to the throater's hand.

The man exchanged looks with both of them, then picked up the coin. Bit it. Eyed them again. Perhaps Johnis's ploy was working after all. Thomas's words during fight school rang in Silvie's ears: "When you deal with a throater, put on the skin of a throater. They are too stupid to respect anything other than arrogance."

"Real gold," the man said, placing the coin on the counter. "You do realize that this one coin is worth more than that Chevy out there. What makes you think I shouldn't just take this from you now?"

"Because you know that something's not normal with us. We're smaller than you and have half your muscle, but we act as though we can wipe the floor with your guts. And we act that way because we know it's true. Show him, Silvie."

A dozen thoughts raced through her mind. She grabbed one out of thin air and put as much bite behind it as she could muster.

"I don't want to hurt the poor fellow," she said.

Johnis, who now stood a step ahead of her, turned back, and for the first time she saw that his face was red. "Show him. Or do you want me to show him?"

He was furious. Anger was pushing him to confront the man.

"Show him how?" she asked.

"With your knife. Cut off one of his earrings or something! Or should I do it?"

"You'd miss and rip out his cheek! Why the aggression toward me? I've done nothing!"

"Then just *show* him! We walk in here and make a simple request in good spirits, and he treats us like we're dogs!"

Silvie was right: Johnis's entire ploy had been born out of rage toward the man, not some crafty ploy to persuade him. He'd risked their necks because of his need to satisfy his anger?

"How dare you!" she snapped.

"What? How dare I what?"

"You're more interested in making a point with this fool than protecting me or finding the books."

She could see by his sudden stillness that she'd connected with him. For a moment they just stared at each other.

"Sorry," he said. Then to the tattooed man, "Sorry, she's right. If you'll just show us how to ride the Chevy, we could save you the

pain of learning what a mistake it is to cross Johnis and Silvie—
or any member of the Forest Guard, for that matter."

The man's face remained fixed for a moment; then a hint of
smile nudged the corner of his mouth. "You guys are a real trip."
The smile flattened. He flipped the coin back toward Johnis.
"Out. Now."

The doorbell clanged, and a visitor walked in, eyed them once
over, dropped what appeared to be two square leaves on the counter,
and walked out, not bothering to give them a second glance.

"That's the feed for these steeds?" Johnis asked.

"Look, enough's enough, dude. You've done your crazy show,
now hit the road before I lose my good nature. Don't push it."

But they'd already pushed it. It would be a mistake to retreat
without playing this hand to the end. Regardless of why Johnis
had pushed things this far, he'd been quite brave. Silvie plucked
the coin from his hand and walked gracefully up to the counter,
aware of the man's eyes on her as she approached him.

She smiled and held the coin up between thumb and forefinger
to keep his eyes from wandering. "Answer a few questions and you
can keep it. Just a few questions and we leave. It's worth your while."

She winked.

The man's blush was nearly imperceptible. Silvie set the coin
before him and leaned on the counter.

"My lover is right, you know," she said, wanting to make it
clear that she was taken. She withdrew her right knife and twirled
it in her fingers. "We can do a few things."

And then, so that he would remain off balance, she whipped the blade toward Johnis with a hard flick of her wrist.

The knife flashed through the air, severed a single lock of hair next to his right ear, and thudded into a carton with the phrase *Diet Coke* printed boldly on its side.

A brown liquid spewed at the tip of the blade and pooled on the floor.

"What's your name?" Silvie asked the man.

"Ray."

"Well, Ray, I think Johnis wants to know how to make one of these car things go. Isn't that right, Johnis?"

"Yes," Johnis said, walking up to the counter. "Tell us that and you can keep the coin."

"You guys are serious? You don't know how to drive?"

"We throw knives, we kill Scabs, we put fools in their place, but we don't drive," Johnis said. "Not yet."

Ray humphed, picked up the coin, and rounded the counter. "You're both nuts."

He led them from the station, explaining that the "feed," as they called it, was actually gas, and the buggies, or more properly "cars," had motors that made them run as long as you kept the tank full of fuel. He showed them how to operate one of the upright feeding troughs, called a "pump."

Johnis took it all in with supreme confidence, though Silvie doubted he was retaining as much as he let on. Then again, he seemed completely taken by the whole business.

When they approached the red Chevy parked next to the station, his eyes stared like a spider's and his jaw remained slightly parted in dumb wonder. Silvie was more taken by his reaction to the contraption than by the car itself.

"Fantastic!" Johnis breathed, stepping lightly around the car. "Cherry Chevy. How long have they been around?"

"Chevys? You can't be serious. You guys really haven't seen a car before? You grow up in a monastery in Tibet or something?"

"Something like that." Johnis held out his hand. "How old is this one?"

"2008."

"Can I touch it?"

"Long as you don't scratch it. The boss has won his share of races in this. Modified. I'm a Harley guy, but I don't mind saying she's a beauty."

Johnis let his fingers run along the dark red skin. "Fantastic. It's like silk!" Silvie followed his example, impressed by the hard shell. She was still more fascinated by him than this cherry.

The attendant opened the doors and let them both sit inside, talking them through the "fundamentals of driving," as he called them. "Insert and turn the key to start it, like this. Put it in Drive. Most street racers are manual, but Joe likes the automatic. That's the brake to stop it. That's the gas to make it go. You steer with the wheel."

"Fantastic!" Johnis stared at the wheel in his hands, ran his fingers over the workings on the black dash, kneaded the leather-wrapped gear stick. It was enough to make Silvie jealous!

"Okay, come on, that's it. Out. I have a customer."

Johnis crawled out, then stuck his head back in and took one last long look. "Where's the key?"

"That wasn't part of the deal. You mess with this car and you'll be sorry you were ever born. In case they didn't teach you this in Tibet, knives don't do too well against shotguns."

The man left them at the door, and they headed behind the building.

"Come on," Johnis said, running back up the hill. He slid to the ground over the top of the hill and spun back on his elbows, giving him a full view of the Texon station below.

"Now what?" Silvie demanded, dropping in beside him.

"Did you feel that skin, Silvie? The smell of the leather, the smooth lines of that body—"

"It's a mechanical beast, not a woman!" she whispered.

"I *have* to have this Chevy!"

"There are hundreds—"

"No. I have to have the cherry Chevy." Johnis tried to explain, stumbling over his own words. "It's a dangerous thing, this driving . . . This is the only car I've touched . . . I know where the levers are . . . It's calling me, Silvie." Then in a stern voice, "We have priorities. We have to get to the Books of History, for the love of Elyon! We're wasting time here!"

He jumped to his feet.

"Where are you going?"

"Wait for me by the Chevy. I'll meet you there."

"No, Johnis, not without me. You can't leave me!"

"I have to get the keys! Meet me by the Chevy!"

"He has a shotgun . . ."

Johnis plunged over the slope. "What's a shotgun? I need that Chevy!"

And then he was racing down the sandy hill.

three

"No change?"

"You speak as though I should know more than you. I expected more considering your power."

"The moment you stop watching the girl is the moment you become useless to me. Is this difficult to understand?"

"Forgive me," she said. "Meeting here, below the earth, among the dead in Romania, affects my judgment. No change."

He held her in a steady glare.

"And the others?" she asked.

"They'll show up eventually. When they do, I have a feeling the whole world will know about it."

"How so?"

"They're not the quiet type."

"Foolish."

"No, *chosen*," he said. "Which makes them as dangerous as they are loud."

"Then we'll just have to shut them up, won't we?"

four

Silvie crouched beside the Chevy, peering through both windows at the gas station's front entrance. The doors to the car were locked, but even if she'd found them open, she wouldn't have dared to enter the small space alone. Johnis might have found a new love in this Chevy, but to her it was still a pile of leather and metal and strange smells, finely crafted or not.

"Come on, Johnis," she muttered. Her nerves had her fidgeting like a young girl. He'd been gone too long! "Come on, come on! I knew it! He's in trouble."

She had to do something. Silvie stood and was about to run for the glass door when it slammed wide and spit Johnis out in a full sprint.

A horrendous boom shook the air, and the glass door shattered.

Johnis's feet slid on the flat concrete as he spun through his turn. Then he was pelting for her, arms pumping like batons.

The Chevy chirped like a bird, and Silvie jumped.

"Mount it!" Johnis cried. "Inside, get inside!"

Silvie jerked the lever that operated the door, flung the contraption wide, and piled in. The car had unlocked on its own?

Ray rushed from the station, bearing what appeared to be a long stick. A shotgun. If the weapon in his arm was responsible for the shattering glass, they were in trouble. Her knives were worthless in such a tiny space!

She nearly dove back out, but Johnis was there, jerking his door open. "He won't harm the Chevy!" he screamed. "You can't put a scratch on the car, can you, Ray?"

The shopkeeper used the shotgun again. Twin blasts of fire belched into the air, chased by a thundering volley. But he'd held the weapon high.

"Don't touch it!" he roared. "I'll fill your backsides so full of lead you won't be able to stand straight."

Johnis dove in and slammed the door shut. He fumbled with a small metal object, searched for the hole that Ray had pointed out earlier as being the ignition.

"I ran into some trouble," he panted.

"Really? And it doesn't look to be over."

"He won't hurt the car."

"He's coming . . ."

The man was storming toward them, shotgun cradled in his arm.

"He's coming, Johnis!"

Johnis wasn't having luck with the key, so he pulled it back and pushed at several small buttons on a black knob attached to the device's metal portion.

The car suddenly chirped again and the locks *clacked* shut.

Johnis looked at her, unable to hide his smirk. "Fantastic . . ."

A hand slammed on his window. "Out!" the tattooed man thundered. "Get out before I blast this door open!"

"He can't! He won't!" Johnis ignored the man and went back to work on the key, this time with more deliberate concentration.

Ray was cursing bitterly, but Johnis was right; he couldn't risk damaging the car. They were safe in this cocoon—for the moment. But they would face even greater danger when an overzealous Johnis got the contraption moving.

"This doesn't look good, Johnis!"

"He's a stubborn thug!"

"What were you thinking?"

The man stood outside the car, voice muted, message clear.

"You're dead meat! You can either get out now, and I might send you off with a good kick in the behind. Or you can make me go back in for the other set of keys, but if I do that, I'm going to take it out on you. You hear me?" He slammed his palm against the window to drive his point home.

Silvie felt like a small child cowering under a monster. "He's got another set of keys?"

The man whirled around and stormed off, leaving a trail of furious words behind him.

"He's got another set of keys! Stop fumbling with that thing and get us out of here!"

"I'm trying, but I can't see . . ."

She grabbed the key from him, lined it up as she saw it must go, and slid it into the hole. Without a second thought, she twisted the key as their instructor had shown them earlier.

The Chevy roared and she jerked back.

Music boomed, louder than she could bear. Not just any music, but the sound of a man screaming, as if the musician was trapped in the motor and was protesting in no uncertain terms.

"Turn it off!" She jabbed at the buttons and controls on the dash. "Stop it!"

Her knuckle must have hit something right, because the music halted as abruptly as it had begun.

Johnis sat frozen. Both hands hovering over the steering wheel, enraptured or terrified or both.

"Here he comes!" The man was running back toward them with a key dangling from his right hand.

Johnis dropped his right hand onto the shift lever and jerked it back. The Chevy started to roll.

He gripped the leather wheel, knuckles white, staring ahead like a shocked monkey.

"Faster!" she cried, seeing the man close on them, sprinting now.

"Careful, careful!" She jabbed her finger at the building to the right. "Watch the stable. Don't run into the hill! Watch—"

"Silence!" Johnis shouted. "I'm trying to drive the Chevy!"

The man was on top of them, banging his palm on the window, cursing obscenely in words that made no sense to Silvie—but she understood the language of his red face clearly enough.

He used the shotgun again, jolting them both.

"Faster, faster!" They were going no faster to escape this monster than if they'd taken a leisurely stroll.

"Okay, okay!" Johnis leaned back, took a quick look at the levers on the floor, then pressed one with his foot.

The Chevy stopped abruptly.

"The other one!"

The car surged forward, effectively silencing them both. Like a rock flung from a slingshot, they sped across the ground and past the stables, heading directly for the sharp incline behind the station.

It was dark, but the moon was full, and Silvie could see clearly enough the metal fencing between them and the hill.

"Stop, stop; turn, turn!"

But Johnis did not stop. He'd frozen, like a boy on his first rope swing, swaying beneath the tall trees near Middle.

"Johnis!" Silvie grabbed the wheel and jerked it hard.

The Chevy spun wildly to the right. Its wheels squealed in protest. They narrowly missed a head-on collision with the fencing and were now racing beside it.

"Let go; I have it!" Johnis cried. Another fence cut across their path ahead, and seeing it, he yanked the wheel as Silvie had done.

The Chevy spun again, but this time it didn't stop spinning. Johnis kept the wheel turned, forcing the car into an arc that filled the air with smoke.

The force shoved Silvie against him. "Straighten!"

Johnis flung the wheel in the opposite direction. The Chevy shot forward, this time headed for the upright pumps . . . and the red-faced attendant standing in front of the pumps.

"Stop!"

"No, no!" Having mastered the skill of turning the Chevy, Johnis opted instead for pulling the wheel to his left. They blasted by the man, who had thrown himself to the ground. Another car was entering the station, and Johnis narrowly avoided a collision.

So he could turn the thing, but could he stop it? Silvie felt her own feet instinctively smashing into the floor, wishing to slow the contraption down.

"Slow down, please! You're going to get us killed!"

"He's back there . . ."

"You're headed for a ditch! You have to stop. Stop!"

But it was too late. They slammed into a shallow ditch, bounced over the other side, and ripped through a fence she hadn't seen. Then they were on a bumpy, hard-packed dirt path instead of the flat roads of rock that the other cars seemed to prefer.

Johnis shifted his foot to the second lever and pushed. They came to a sliding halt. Dust floated past them.

Silence.

"Fantastic!"

Silvie punched his arm, furious that he'd put them in this predicament. "This isn't a child's game! Stop it with the 'fantastic' every other moment!"

"But you have to admit: it's like riding a hundred horses at once. Imagine going to battle with the Horde in one of these."

"There's no room to maneuver your sword."

"We'd use a shotgun."

They looked at each other, then twisted back for a view of the station. Sure enough, the shotgun-bearing man named Ray was already halfway across the station in a full sprint.

"Fool," Johnis said and shoved his foot on the gas lever. The Chevy spun its wheels in the dirt, then shot into the night.

Johnis managed to keep the car on the path, careening from side to side as he wrestled the wheel. But they were speeding away from the station, and that was good for Silvie.

"You can stop it if you have to, right?"

"Sure." To demonstrate, Johnis hit the brake, and the Chevy went into a slide that piled them both up on his side.

"See?"

"Does this thing not know the meaning of gentle? This whole world appears to be violent."

"Don't be ridiculous. She can glide like a feather if I tell her to."

"Now it's a she?"

Johnis took off again, this time slowly at first, then gaining speed as they bounded down the road.

"Put her on the proper road and she will glide, I can promise you that," he said breathlessly. "Fantastic, I'm telling you. Mind-blowing."

"Just drive safely. Keep your eyes on the path. Why does this one not have lamps to guide us, like the other ones?"

"Start punching buttons and you'll find them. But then we'll be seen."

He had a good point.

"They'll be coming for us, you do realize that?"

His face lost some of its boyish delight. "Yes. But we have the Chevy, and we have the night. It's a good start, Silvie."

"It could also be a good end."

five

The moon stood over them, round and bright, watching their every move. They'd brought the car to a stop a hundred yards off the dirt road in a shallow, sandy wash that protected them.

Johnis led them both in a detailed exploration of the Chevy by moonlight, and now, out of harm's way, Silvie found herself caught up in his excitement.

They'd run through a whole gamut of exercises in an attempt to find the lamps on the Chevy and succeeded in triggering everything but. The music, the rear compartment door, sticks that presumably cleaned the front window, lights that blinked orange, even a loud horn that sent Silvie diving for cover when Johnis leaned on it.

If they were going to venture onto the big road with the other Chevys, they had to use their lamps, no question. Johnis was bent over the front, looking for an exterior switch that might ignite them, when Silvie twisted the lever that moved the window cleaning sticks when pushed.

Twin lights blazed into Johnis's face.

"Ahh!" He jumped back and threw his arm over his eyes. The light reached past him and illuminated the sandy slope beyond.

Slowly Johnis lowered his arm. A broad grin split his face. "Yes! You've done it!" He twisted and stared at the far-reaching beams. "Fantastic! Look at that, will you?"

Silvie jumped out, ran to the front, and leaped into the dazzling shafts of light. "Whoo-hoo!" She grabbed his hands and they danced in a circle like children, carrying on as if they'd just heard news that the Horde had laid down their swords for good.

"What did I say?" Johnis cried.

"I don't know, what did you say?"

"I don't know, but it's fantastic."

"We made it." Silvie stared into Johnis's eyes, smiling wide with him. "You were right, my handsome warrior. We've crossed the worlds and taken the enemy's treasured Chevy from under his nose, and now we've conquered it."

"Yes, we have."

Their dancing slowed.

"I owe you my life," she said.

They were only partly serious in this mood of frivolity, but the nature of that mood was shifting quickly. They circled each other, arms stretched, hands clasped.

"I owe you *my* life," Johnis said.

Silvie felt her stomach lighten, her heart swell. The world slowed around them.

"Did you mean what you said?" Johnis asked. "To the attendant?"

The statement about him being her lover had stayed in the back of Silvie's mind, but not until now, staring into his eyes, did she understand how much she longed for the statement to be true.

"Should I have meant it?" she asked, sliding her hands up his arms.

The last of Johnis's smile faded. His boyish charm was gone, replaced by a gaze of deep longing. His eyes swallowed her, like windows into a new world—a world that could be a sanctuary of perfect peace and love.

He stepped into her arms and enfolded her in his embrace. His head tilted slightly to one side, and he pulled her to himself. His soft lips pressed lightly against hers. Then he bit her lower lip tenderly, and she felt her mind spin.

This was Johnis, the man who had led her into terrible danger, to the brink of death, alongside impossible odds, for the sake of love and loyalty—the chosen one who'd never faltered or strayed from the way of his heart.

This was the man she'd fallen madly in love with. Having that love returned now sealed her own longing. Silvie pressed against him and passionately returned his embrace. They kissed long and tenderly, hearts pounding against each other's chests.

Other sixteen-year-olds in Middle were joining in marriage, but she and Johnis had crossed worlds to find their love. And nothing could possibly be sweeter. When she pulled away from him, she half-expected the night to have passed, but the sky was still black, and the Chevy's lamps still drilled the darkness with its two beams of brilliant light.

Johnis was breathing steadily. He smiled and drew her close again. "I've dreamed of that longer than you know."

"You have?"

"From the moment I saw you fighting over the Horde ball in Middle, I wondered what it would be like to kiss you."

"Then it's not just the air here?"

"No," he said and kissed her again. "Definitely not, although the air does seem to loosen things up a bit, doesn't it?"

"Just a bit." She smiled, and they kissed yet again.

A thumping sound joined her heart, like a muted drum in the sky. The sound jerked her back to earth.

"What's that?"

They scrambled to the top of the knoll on their right and saw the source of the beating—a bird or flying car, moving across the horizon slowly, shining a light onto the road they'd traveled. Lights from cars racing toward the city stretched out along the big road beyond.

"They're looking for us!" she said. "They'll see the lamps!"

Johnis spun and raced back to the car. "How did you ignite them?"

She slid into the seat next to him and turned the lamps off. "Now what?"

"They're following the same road we did. We wait for them to pass us, then head back in the dark, join the other cars on the big road, and take the Chevy to Las Vegas."

Silvie thought about his plan, which sounded more like a vague notion than a reasoned course of action. But she felt emboldened with the taste of his lips lingering on her own.

"Assuming we survive the other Chevys and make it to this Las Vegas, then what?"

"The attendant mentioned an arena for fighters called the Excalibur. Dangerous perhaps, but I think we would fit in. We start there. And we find Darsal and Karas before the Dark One does."

"Assuming Alucard hasn't found them already."

THE BIG ROAD WAS A NIGHTMARE IN THE MAKING; SILVIE could see that much as Johnis angled the Chevy down the strip that merged with cars racing east.

He'd learned to maneuver the car fairly well on the dirt road, but his confidence was challenged by the sight ahead: not the road but the other cars.

"Lights!"

He ignited them, then pulled out onto the road. A horn blared behind as a car swerved to avoid running up their backside.

"Patience!" Johnis snapped at the passing Chevy.

"Easy, just keep us on the road. Ignore them."

"How can I? They're traveling like lightning past us. I have to speed up."

He fed the Chevy more gas, and they flew down the road. Another car blasted them, blaring a rude horn, and Johnis took his speed even higher. Cars were still passing them but not as if they were stopped. Slowly his confidence returned, and he increased their speed.

The next fifteen minutes raced by without event. The road was flat, straight as an arrow. But the moment they crested the last hill and caught their first close-up view of the city called Las Vegas, the complexity of their journey increased tenfold.

For starters, the number of cars seemed to have doubled without warning, forcing Johnis to concentrate on all sides, careful not to run into a slowing Chevy ahead yet staying in front of the impatient Chevys behind. He repeatedly braked hard, then zoomed forward with enough suddenness to tear an unprepared passenger's head from his shoulders.

"Slow down!"

A horn blared behind.

"And be run over?" Johnis muttered angrily and swerved into the space to his left, then shot past the car that had slowed before them. He shook his fist at the man as he sped by.

Two minutes later the same car drove past them, its rider glaring angrily.

"You see what happens when you lose your patience?" Silvie snapped.

"He's a menace!"

The increase in cars was made even more complicated by the sheer magnitude of the city they approached. Las Vegas was lit up like the stars, only far brighter and brimming with red, blue, and golden hues that shone like jewels.

The enormity of it all made it hard for either of them to keep their undivided attention on the Chevys around them.

The roads widened, and soon thousands of lights streamed by on all sides. The city of lights. How would they ever find this festival called "Excalibur"? But none of this prepared them for the final complexity that suddenly altered their relatively successful experience in the Histories thus far.

"Lights, everywhere lights," Johnis cried. "I can't see straight for all the lights. Now red and blue lights on top of a Chevy are riding our tail. We have to get out and find our bearings."

Silvie twisted in her seat and saw the car behind them, red and blue lights flashing on its roof. The driver . . .

She gasped.

"What?"

"He's a warrior. In uniform! He . . . he's motioning us to the side!"

"You're sure?"

A *blurp* sounded from the car, a horn of some kind, but this one didn't end. It wailed, rising and falling in a sound that sent chills down Silvie's spine.

"They're looking at us," Johnis said.

"Who is?"

"Everyone!"

And drawing aside, Silvie saw. Not unlike herding hunters pulling wide to give the archer plenty of space for a shot at the prey.

"He's after us, Johnis!" Panic swelled through her mind. "Go! Run for your life! Get us out of here!"

The Chevy surged forward. Johnis whipped the car around a white one and left it to deal with the hunter behind them. As if they needed any confirmation that they were indeed being hunted, the Chevy with flashing lights veered around the same white car and closed quickly.

"Dear Elyon, help us!" he cried and wound the motor higher.

"Faster."

"I'm going faster!"

"It's a race car; make it race!"

Johnis set his jaw the way he had heading into the Black Forest and the Horde city or a dozen other occasions when he'd thrown caution to the wind in favor of principle.

Gripping the wheel with both fists, he swerved first to the left around a third car, then all the way across to the right, racing past the Chevys as if it were now they who were standing still.

"Careful . . ." Silvie cut herself short, thinking that he was actually mastering the Chevy with surprising ease.

The hunter behind had been joined by a second, both wailing as they gave pursuit. "Never mind, go! There!" She pointed at a large green sign that read LAS VEGAS BOULEVARD.

Johnis swerved for the road under the sign and flew down the slope, blaring his own horn to warn the slowing cars to move out of his way.

An obstacle they hadn't yet seen presented itself ahead: red lights hanging over the road. A dozen Chevys had stopped under them as if facing an invisible wall.

"Johnis . . ."

"Navigate!" he cried. "We can't stop; the hunters are gaining. Find a hole, tell me . . ." His intense concentration stopped him, but she knew that he was right. They were in a Horde city from the Histories, being hounded by two warriors or hunters who undoubtedly meant to kill them.

If they were to survive and go after the books . . .

"To the right!" The opening was narrow, between two cars, and she couldn't see beyond, but it was the only gap she could see.

"Over the lip?"

"What lip?"

Johnis shot for the gap to their right, and Silvie saw Johnis's "lip" then: a thin fence bordered the road, then gave way to a cliff beyond.

"Johnis!"

But Johnis was flying faster. They cut the car on their right off, forcing its rider into a squealing brake. It was all a blur now, and Silvie threw her arms up to protect her face.

The Chevy hit a curb and launched up, nose high in the air. Then they were airborne.

"Hold on . . ."

"Dear Elyon, save us!"

They sailed ten yards and landed level with a horrendous crash, bounced once, then flew forward on spinning wheels.

They'd survived?

Unscathed, it would seem, but the car was now screaming directly for another line of cars stopped beneath a line of hanging red lights.

To this point Johnis had managed to maneuver the Chevy down the mountain and into the city without touching another car. Seeing the line, Silvie knew that would now change. She braced herself for the impact.

Johnis whipped the wheel to his left, slammed his foot on the brake, then released it and applied more gas. The Chevy went into a broad slide, then abruptly straightened, flying past the line of stopped cars.

Horns blared. The Chevy missed all but the last car, which was pulled out halfway through a right-hand turn.

"Watch it . . ."

The impact came along Silvie's door, a loud clash of metal against metal. Sparks flew. More horns blared.

And then they were through, up over a curb, clipping a tree trunk, and back on the road.

Clear.

"You okay?" Johnis asked.

"Yes. We did it?"

"We caused a ruckus. They all stopped, but they'll be after us, that's for sure."

The rising and falling horns of the warriors in pursuit wailed through the Chevy's carriage.

"By the sounds of it, a whole horde of them are after us." Silvie tried to calm the trembling in her hands but failed to.

"I think we should leave this car."

"No, no, no, we can't leave the Chevy. It's . . ." Johnis's eyes darted about, blinking at the towering lights by the road, then behind in the mirror. "You're right. You're right, we're too obvious."

Silvie settled enough to take in the lights that rose on both sides—an incredible display of reds and greens and every color of the rainbow. Massive squares the size of whole buildings were painted with moving faces and pictures.

She couldn't make sense of anything she saw. Terrifying.

"Fantastic," Johnis muttered.

Silvie twisted back and saw not one, not two, not four or six sets of flashing lights, but a dozen, racing up the empty road behind them.

"We have company."

"We have to leave the Chevy. I see it; hold tight."

Johnis whipped the car to the right through a crossroad that led to a massive pyramid structure. The sign read EXCALIBUR.

"See what?" Silvie demanded, looking back to see if the warriors had seen them make the turn.

"Excalibur. Hold on!" Johnis jerked the wheel hard, throwing her into the door. The car careened into a dark alley. They clipped a large green bin and slid to a stop. He killed the motor and extinguished the lamps.

The motor ticked in the sudden quiet. He looked at Silvie, eyes wide, face beaded with sweat.

"What do you think?"

The warriors' Chevys wailed with increasing intensity.

"I think they saw us turning," Silvie said.

They moved as one, each shoving open a door and scrambling out. The wailing from the cars in pursuit was now on top of them. Johnis grabbed her hand and pulled her into a sprint down the alley—away from their Chevy.

Toward the Excalibur.

Six

The Excalibur was built like a castle, with red and purple spires lit brightly against the black sky. Massive. Everything in the Histories was colossal. And as brilliant as a colored sun.

They ran side by side, their feet pounding with the roar of the city—noise, noise, everywhere noise! It was as if sun had been captured by the Horde and was now hooked into this city called Las Vegas. The burning smell was enough to make Silvie blanch, though she suspected the odor came from the cars, not the buildings.

They saved their breath, but Silvie was too astonished by the sights and sounds and smells to speak intelligently. Having been stranded in a strange world only to find company in such frightful things as warriors screaming about in Chevys and mountains of lights that flashed overhead without pause, she was a twisted knot of mangled nerves.

She grabbed Johnis's hand as they approached a flight of stairs leading into the Excalibur and pulled him to a stop, barely winded despite their fast run.

A steady river of people flowed in and out of a dozen glass doors. They stood on the landing between the Excalibur and Las Vegas Boulevard, breathing hard.

"Good night! You ever hear so many sirens?" a large redheaded man exclaimed, facing the street. "That ambulances or police?"

"Cops," said a shorter fellow wearing a sleeveless tunic and baggy shorts. "Some crash has the traffic piled up at Tropicana."

Johnis pulled Silvie forward, then released her hand and took steps two at a time. Silvie glanced back and saw no immediate threat. Their best option was to enter a crowd and lose themselves. The authorities knew the city and would quickly cut off any avenue of escape. But if they could lose themselves inside the hunter's net while they came to terms with their predicament, they stood a strong chance of slipping through that net later.

If they were to take Ray, the bald gas man, at his suggestion, they should fit in at the Excalibur. *Smart*, she agreed. But seeing Johnis rush up the steps now, she wasn't sure they would fit in. None of the other guests wore battle leather or tunics similar to their own. Boots clacked on the stone behind her, and she twisted back to see five blue-suited warriors running past a fountain fifty yards away.

"Johnis . . ." She bounded up the steps and passed him near the top. "They've seen us! Hurry!"

They spun through the doors into a world even more frightening than the one outside: hundreds of machines situated in long rows, green-clothed tables, lighted wheels. The sheer number of people and the horrendous crash of bells and gongs made her head spin.

"Excuse me."

Silvie turned to her right. A warrior in a brown shirt, bearing a club and a weapon in a waist sheath.

"Knives aren't permitted in the main casino. You'll have to take the fighter's entrance on the west side."

Silvie crouched and touched the knife on her right thigh. The warrior's demeanor changed the moment her fingers made contact with the bone handle. Had she made a mistake?

For a moment neither of them moved. And then the guard lifted a black box to his mouth and issued orders. The man waited a second, and the box spoke back to him: "On our way."

"Follow me!" Johnis whispered.

He ran over a soft red floor, woven cotton perhaps, past what he now saw were gaming tables, not so different from the more rudimentary betting cages that some of the Forest Guard played to waste their time between battles.

"Stop!"

Johnis flew through the aisles, and Silvie stayed hard on his heels. They raced the full length of one aisle before he cut sharply to his left and ran directly into a long table surrounded by eight players.

He could have stopped in time to avoid a collision, but in this state of anxiety dove over the table, landed on his hands, and rolled to his feet.

So Silvie dove as well. With all of her might, she launched herself into the air, soared ten feet, and landed on her hands as he had. She rolled to her feet and plowed into Johnis.

He staggered back a step, but his eyes were on the table. Stunned by what they'd just done with surprising ease.

"After me." He sprinted to his right, glancing up. Silvie now saw what had caused him to turn in the first place: a sign bearing a warrior dressed in fighting leathers, armed with a sword.

CLASH OF THE GLADIATORS

They'd lost the guard and whatever reinforcements had come to his aide, and they'd done so with surprising speed. But Silvie didn't have time to dwell on this small accomplishment at the moment. They were like two rats on a king's banquet table; expecting to dash around from dish to dish without being soundly smashed and fed to the dogs was the stuff of fancy.

Johnis ducked into a hallway marked by the CLASH OF THE GLADIATORS sign and slowed to a fast walk. Silvie glanced back down the aisles as they rounded the corner. Three guards raced into the aisle a hundred yards behind.

She leaped into the hall. "They're still coming!"

The hall they had entered was bordered with several white doors

marked by lighted signs that made no sense to her: AUTHORIZED
PERSONNEL ONLY. The hall ended at a red wall with a large picture of a stately looking fellow wearing a crown on his head.

"Find an open door." Johnis was already trying the handles.

"It's a dead end, Johnis!" She stepped across the hall and tried
two of the doors—both locked.

The guard's boots pounded down the aisles.

"Johnis!" she whispered. "This is nothing! We have to get out
of here!" Panic crowded her throat. They were trapped rats!

Johnis tried the other doors and found them all locked. Silvie
grabbed his elbow. "We're going to have to fight them." She
flipped a knife into her left palm. "If it doesn't go well, I want you
to know that I love you. I always have."

The door behind them suddenly flew open, and a short, fat
man with ruddy cheeks and cropped blond hair that had tinges of
red in it held the door wide. He looked surprised to see them.

"Gladiators?"

Johnis hesitated only a moment, then shoved Silvie forward.
"Finally!"

They hurried past the man into a dark hall that ran to a lighted
door. "All participants use the west entrance, man," the fellow said
after them. "Second door on your right." Then he dipped back
out the door, leaving them alone.

From somewhere to their left a crowd roared. They looked to
be in the innards of the building, behind the arena—this Clash of
Gladiators. But for the moment they were safe.

"Did they see us?"

Silvie didn't have to answer. Muffled cries reached them from beyond the door they'd just entered. "This way! This way!"

Johnis and Silvie ran down the hall, flew into the second doorway to their right, and slid to a stop in front of a long row of uniforms.

"Dress, hurry!" Johnis dashed to the line of battle dress and quickly shrugged into a red cape.

There were three things that all Forest Dwellers held in the highest regard, things Thomas of Hunter, their supreme commander, reminded them of often: their ferocity in battle, their gentleness in love, and their enthusiasm in celebrating at the end of a long day of both.

The celebrations consisted of all forms of song, dance, and the spinning of tales. And playacting brought it all together.

"Is this for real or is it a game?" Silvie asked.

"This, or that?" Johnis indicated the crowd's roar from beyond the walls.

"That," Silvie said.

"Killing for mere sport seems a bit barbaric, but this is the Histories."

"Then this costume is ridiculous. Are we doing this to blend in or to fight? Because it won't help our fighting."

"I have no intention of fighting," Johnis said, pulling on a metal helmet. "Hurry."

Silvie threw on a cape like his, then a large metal helmet that covered her head like a gong. If they did get into a fight, the first order of business would be to ditch it.

"Good," Johnis said, looking her over. "It'll slow them down."

"And us," she said.

"Just till we get out of here."

He led her quickly through the armory. Leather and metal fighting dress. Knives and mallets and swords. Enough armor and weaponry to outfit a whole division.

Silvie snatched up a sword and spun it in her hand. A long steel blade with a handle formed from wood. Not the best craftsmanship, and the blade was duller than she liked, but the balance was decent. For the first time since entering the fireball called Las Vegas, she felt a measure of confidence.

Johnis grabbed a sword and rushed forward without bothering to scrutinize it. Silvie had spent some time showing him the finer points of swordplay, and he was improving rapidly, but the lust for battle wasn't what made Johnis great.

He tried a side door, found it open, and ducked in. Silvie followed him into what turned out to be a small white room with half a dozen stall doors and a row of white stone basins. Mirrored glass hung on one wall, reflecting them in their red capes and helmets.

"A bathroom." Johnis's voice echoed.

"Clearly."

They stood undecided for a few breaths. The guards would now be coming through the armory. They were running out of time. Only one reasonable option.

"Hide!"

Silvie was halfway to the row of stalls when the main door pushed open. A man dressed in black slacks and a black shirt with a face that looked too long for the tuft of hair perched on its crown snapped at Johnis. "Enough heaving, man, it's getting started."

Then he saw Silvie, who stood facing them both. A grin twisted his white cheeks. "Oh, I get it. Save it for later, man."

"She comes too," Johnis said.

"You wish. Let's go."

They could either play along with this dimwit or take him out and face the guard. Clearly they should do the former.

"Wait here," Johnis said to her. "I'll be right back."

"What? What are you talking about?"

He stepped closer and spoke in a hurried hush. "They're coming! We can't risk a disturbance. We have to blend. Hide in the stalls; I'll break away as soon as I can."

"Johnis!" The thought of separating from him filled her with a bone-jarring dread. "I can't!"

"You have to!"

He spun back to the man who was plastered with a knowing grin. "Okay, let's go."

She watched him walk out. The man with the long face winked. Watched the door swing shut with a *whoosh*. And all the while she could not move.

Johnis had left her.

The sound of running boots reached her from somewhere in the armory. *He was right; if we'd tried to make a run for it, we would have run into the guard.*

The sound of the cheering crowd swelled. *Johnis doesn't know what he's getting himself into!*

Rushing water swirled in the stall on the bathroom's far side. *I'm not alone.*

seven

The moment Johnis stepped into the doorway, he realized that he'd walked into a trap.

They walked onto a field similar in some ways to the stadium in Middle where they'd played with the Horde ball. Where challenges were made and fought. Bright lights lit an arena fifty yards in width. At the center rose a platform and a gallows. A circle of twenty warriors stood at attention around the platform.

The stands were filled with thousands of onlookers who'd gathered for the fight. An earsplitting roar swelled as the door behind Johnis closed. "Fight, fight, fight, fight! Kill, kill, kill, kill!" The chant rose to a crescendo.

He instinctively backed into the door, tried the handle, and found it locked. The walls that surrounded the arena rose ten feet before meeting rings of benches that ran the arena's circumference. No doors, no halls, no ladders.

This wasn't good. He'd left Silvie, knowing that the guards were looking for two people who didn't belong. Making a fuss in the bathroom would have only attracted attention. The guard had rushed past the bathroom just behind him. So his play had bought them a breath or two.

But none of this calmed his heart.

"It's a good day to die," the man said. He stepped behind a tall gate, locked it, and walked into a booth with bars.

When Johnis looked back at the platform, the warriors were spreading out in two lines. A quick glance around told him three things that were now as unbendable as the ground itself: One, the crowd was here to see someone fight. And perhaps be killed. Two, that person was him, unless his logic was failing him totally, which could be the case. He'd felt inordinately stupid since his arrival in the Histories—fast on his feet and full of passion but slow in his mind and as jittery as a trembling mouse crossing a table in broad daylight. Three, the crowd *would* see him fight and perhaps be killed because there was no avenue for escape that he could see.

A fighter dressed in black from head to foot, wearing a tight-fitting black hood, stood tall on the platform and clapped his hands three times. The crowd fell silent.

The executioner's voice rang out: "Prisoner, you have been found guilty of fleeing justice and giving aid to the enemy. As is mandated by law, you have been sentenced to death. As is also permitted by law, you may either be hanged by the neck at the gallows until dead, or you may fight to prove your innocence in mortal combat with twenty of the king's guards. Which do you choose?"

Neither, he tried to scream, but his throat remained closed.

"Has the cat nipped your tongue, prisoner?"

Laughter rippled through the crowd.

Johnis stepped forward, weighing his options, which were few, perhaps even nonexistent, in this death chamber. He could try to confound them and buy some time, but doing so would only give the guard more time to find him.

Or he could fight.

His limbs felt numb. This was it, then. He'd crossed the worlds to face his death in a chamber of bloodthirsty, scabless Horde—

Unless . . .

"I choose to speak to the king!" he called out.

"That is not an option."

The warriors he was to fight now stood in rows of ten on each side. The executioner motioned them forward, and they began to advance.

"Then you will have his wrath!" Johnis circled to his right. "I am his cousin, and to kill royalty is death."

His announcement stopped them cold. But not out of fear. Confusion at his audacity, more likely.

He picked up his pace, closer to the soldiers on his right and farther from those on his left. *Better to take them head-on, a few at a time, than broadside, where the whole mass can club you to death.* Silvie had learned the tactic as a child, and had also taught him.

"There's been a mistake! I am not sentenced to death. I was kidnapped on my way to the lake . . . by the Horde . . . who then forced the Chevy that was carrying the prisoner off the road and put me in his place!"

His voice echoed to silence.

"Is that so?"

"That is so! Send for the king; he'll tell you."

Johnis wasn't about to think his nonsensical little tale would earn him any more than a few seconds if the executioner had any wits, but he needed every advantage he could get. His mind spun, considering the odds of his survival in sword fight with twenty warriors.

None.

So what was he to do, kill as many as he could and then take a sword? He hadn't come to the Histories to die in an arena, mistaken for whoever they thought he was!

"You care to entertain us with your stories, is that it?" The executioner demanded, unable to hide the humor in his voice. He spread his arms to the crowd. "What is your verdict? Fight or flight?"

"Fight, fight, fight, fight! Kill, kill, kill, kill!" They'd done this before, in perfect unison. The Horde from the Histories didn't drown their prisoners as the Scabs in his world did.

They forced them into a death match for sport or hung them from the neck until dead.

Johnis tossed his sword far to one side. The crowd stilled to the snap of a twig as the blade arced gracefully through the air and landed in the dust with a dull slap.

"Then let me take any one man, give him a sword, and let me fight him bare-handed," Johnis cried. "If I win, let me go free. Or is that too much for the Horde from the Histories?"

A lone spectator yelled raw from the top of the arena. "Fight the bugger!"

"An entertainer for sure," the executioner said. "Well? Do we have a taker?"

From the far end a single warrior, twice Johnis's size in both thickness and height, stepped from the line and walked out into the open.

He ripped off his helmet with a thick, gnarled hand and dropped it into the dust. "I accept."

SILVIE CONSIDERED TEARING FROM THE BATHROOM THE moment she realized that someone else was in the stall—the party Johnis had been mistaken for.

But now she was alone, and the guard would be intensifying their search. It would be better for her to hide in one of the stalls until Johnis returned, assuming he would. The thought sent a chill down her back.

Silvie stood frozen in a moment of indecision, staring at her mirror image—a red-caped warrior with a ridiculous helmet that was suffocating her. She could hardly see in the thing! So she ripped it off.

Move, Silvie!

She'd taken two steps toward the nearest toilet when the far stall door flew open and a warrior dressed in a red cape stepped out, cleared his throat, and spit to one side. She knew by the widening of his eyes that he hadn't expected to see her standing here looking at him.

"Wrong bathroom," he said.

What was she to say?

"Ladies across the hall."

"Sorry."

His look of shock gave way to a thin grin that snaked over a scarred face. His head was shaven clean, but the helmet he held in his right hand was identical to hers. And he, like she, wore a red cape. He was comparable to Johnis only in his smaller size—she could see how they might be confused for one another—wearing helmets hides their features.

"I didn't know they were going to execute a lass today."

"They're not," she snapped.

"No, you just dressed up like a prisoner for the thrill of it, eh?" Now he was wearing a wicked, yellow-toothed smile that tempted her to slap him hard. Instead, she opted for keeping calm. There were still boots thudding past outside.

Another thought dawned. They'd taken Johnis, thinking he was a prisoner to be executed!

"It's all a mistake." She fought to keep her nerves under control. The man's eyes dropped to her trembling hands. Why couldn't she control herself in this place cursed by Elyon?

"Yes, of course." The man angled for the door, eyes steady on her. He smelled like too much drink mixed with a night of vomiting.

"You're a fighter. I can see it in your lovely little eyes, sweetheart. Gonna take half of them down with you, aren't you? This ain't the Dark Ages, you know: 2020 when they just played around. It's brutal out there. Why don't you let me have some fun before they kill us both?"

"Why don't you take your skinny backside out of here before I put my boot up it?" she retorted. But did she really want to leave an unconscious man on the floor for the guard to find? It would only bring more of them.

The man's grin only widened. "Passion before death and all that. It's all part of the deal, isn't it?"

Silvie suddenly realized that he wasn't intending to head out the door but was circling around to cut off her escape. She needed to distract him.

"Do they execute all prisoners here?"

"Only the ones with the red capes. Unless you manage to *kill* them all. You see, we have nothing to lose." His emphasis on the word *kill* clearly revealed his doubt that it was possible.

Johnis was in terrible trouble . . . A wave of heat spread down her neck. She nearly swatted the bald fool aside and bolted for the door then. But she had no reasonable course that would land her anywhere except in the gallows herself, in no shape to help Johnis.

"Come on, sweetie, what do you say: a kiss before the old death match?"

The door behind the skunk swung wide and filled with a guard. Silvie's line of sight was mostly blocked by the other prisoner, but she could see over his shoulder enough to know that this guard wasn't the same one who'd confronted her at the front doors.

She moved closer. "Now you're talking my language," she said. Then in a whisper, "Don't let him stop us! Kiss me . . ."

The rank-smelling man stepped up and snaked his thin arms around her. His lips smothered hers in a thick, wet kiss.

eight

The crowd sat in perfect silence, not daring to disturb the echo of those two words of invitation they longed to hear: *I accept*.

They would get their fight. And not the twenty-on-one smashing that would be over before it started, but a contest between this unorthodox runt and their Goliath.

Johnis scanned the stadium once again, hoping for an avenue of escape, but only saw doors between the seats up high, and even those were guarded.

The only advantage he might have over the huge warrior who faced him from twenty yards away was speed. One whack from the man's broadsword and Johnis would go down in a sea of blood. Helmet or not.

He lifted his helmet off his head and tossed it to one side. His opponent began to walk toward him.

The chant began like a hum, then swelled to a roar. "Vigor, Vigor, Vigor, Vigor!"

Clearly they had seen Vigor rip the heads from other prisoners' shoulders before and wanted to see the sight again. Two weeks earlier the chant from a different crowd in a different world had been in praise of him, the chosen one, who'd turned the Horde back at the Natalga Gap. The sound of it still rang in his ears: *Johnis, Johnis, Johnis, Johnis!*

"Dear Elyon, help me," he whispered. He wasn't sure if the shaking at the soles of his feet came from the crowd's roar or from his own bones, but he didn't think he'd ever felt quite so desperate as he did now.

It was one thing to face Teeleh, knowing the Roush were there to back you up. But he had no clue what kind of provision existed in the Histories.

"Vigor, Vigor, Vigor, Vigor!"

And then Vigor was lumbering for him, a large sword comfortable in his right hand. Biceps swollen the size of Johnis's whole head. Thigh muscles rippled like a stallion's flank. Worse, the man was no longer lumbering but bounding on the balls of his feet, limber and surprisingly quick.

The notion to dive for his helmet and roll into a tight protective ball entered his mind and was gone before it could be counted as more than a foolish instinct left over from his childhood. But the instinct returned stronger this time. He didn't know what to do. So he just stood still, like a twig planted firmly in the hard soil.

"Vigor, Vigor . . ." The cries softened, then faded altogether as the crowd sensed an outright pummeling—their bull would soon trample this mouse who'd spoken so bravely but now stood quivering in the dust.

Vigor uttered a grunt ten feet away, pulled back his sword (still at a full run), and swung the blade in an arc that Johnis judged would reach his neck at the peak of its momentum.

He waited a full count, then dropped into the protective ball. His body collapsed into itself and fell to the ground like a coiled spring, faster than Vigor could have anticipated.

The warrior's sword swept through empty air, and both feet reached the balled form on the ground, one right after the other. Both stopped at Johnis's midsection.

The rest of Vigor's body, however, was not so quick. It catapulted over Johnis, went airborne—feet high, head low—and sailed ten feet before gravity finally had its way with the man. Johnis watched the whole thing with his face pressed into two inches of dirt.

The *thud* of Vigor's chest and face slamming into ground.

A terrifying *crack* of bone.

The gasp from the crowd.

Johnis breathed hard, nostrils blowing at the dust. It was the only sound he heard in the wake of the mighty fall. Vigor lay still.

Johnis lifted his head and stared at the larger man's closed eyes facing him from a dozen feet away.

The eyes snapped open and stared at him.

Vigor suddenly sprang up to his feet and shook off the fall. But . . . he'd heard a crack! The man's back or his neck.

"Vigor, Vigor, Vigor, Vigor!"

Vigor rushed him.

Too late to rely on anything but raw instinct. Johnis leaped to his feet and ran away from the indestructible monster whose eyes now bulged with fury at the runt who tripped him up.

It took him only a few strides at a full sprint to feel the same surge of power he'd felt racing through the gaming hall. There was something in the air here, he'd thought then. It made him overly zealous. It made him cry. It made him dull in the head at times.

And it made him fast.

Speed might not help him fell the mighty beast named Vigor, but it would help him run away. Johnis flew straight for the line of warriors watching from behind their helmets. He could feel the red cape tug at his neck, and he shrugged out of it.

The executioner stood in his black outfit, arms crossed, atop the platform. Johnis veered to his right and headed for the far side wall. When he reached the wood planking, he angled left and ran parallel, looking back for the first time since leaving them behind.

Vigor was still sprinting toward him. But he was a good fifty yards off. He'd put that much distance on the man?

The crowd had gone quiet. A youthful, high-strung voice spoke what was on Johnis's mind, if not the crowd's. "Man, he's fast!"

Okay, so he was fast. What was he going to do, run around the arena like a chicken with its head cut off? Eventually they would tire of his running and send the rest after him.

He still had the knife strapped to his thigh, but he couldn't afford to lose it on one throw at the man bearing down on him.

Johnis feigned left then took off to his right, sprinting toward the center again, dangerously close to Vigor. Fast with the wind in his hair. Maybe twice as fast as he remembered being able to run.

He sped past the man, headed toward the platform, and veered behind, as if crossing to the far side again.

But he did not cross to the far side. Halfway down the length of the platform he turned into it, cutting as close to a right angle as his speed would allow.

He reached the platform in five streaking strides, launched himself into a dive that cleared the five-foot height, rolled across the platform, and came to his feet beside the executioner.

Before the man had a chance to recover from the brash and speedy transition from flight to fight, Johnis was behind him and had his blade at the man's neck. He slammed the back of the man's knee, dropping him off balance to his haunches.

"Call him off, or I cut your throat where you stand!" he screamed.

Silvie let the bald prisoner kiss her hungrily and waited patiently. He was smelly and wet and reminded her of a slug, but at the moment she would take a slug over captivity.

"Hey! There's a man and woman—"

"Can't you see we're busy here?" the man yelled, ripping his lips from hers. He spun and stared the guard down. "You have a problem with the condemned catching a moment of bliss before death?"

Presumably satisfied that the bald head didn't match the description he'd been given, the guard finally dipped his head and ducked out.

The prisoner came around, a sly grin parting his lips to reveal his smelly yellow teeth. "Now, where were we?"

Unable to tolerate the man a moment longer, Silvie slammed her right knee into the man's groin.

He gasped and doubled over in pain.

"You were begging for this." She brought her left knee up into his face. His nose cracked and he toppled to one side, out cold.

"Never mistake a woman as an opportunity for bliss."

Silvie snatched up her helmet and pulled it on as she fled the room, leaving her sword.

No guards. The crowd's roar came from up ahead. She'd pieced their predicament together well enough by now. The Horde were known to hold public executions in which prisoners were drowned. But sometimes they had sport with the prisoners before their deaths. So it was in the Histories. She and Johnis had stumbled into a public execution, and Johnis had been mistaken as the prisoner who lay unconscious behind her.

She rushed across the room that held the capes that identified prisoners as condemned. A dark passageway ran adjacent the sound of a crowd's roar. A door: locked.

Johnis is behind this door. My lover has been led through this door to the slaughter.

Silvie hefted the helmet off her head and tossed the useless vessel to the side. She raced along the wall, looking for another way past. It rose ten feet and cracked at the top where steel tubes crisscrossed to form girding for a large structure. An auditorium.

The crowd had grown silent. Silvie raced farther into the darkness. The passageway ended in a hallway that ran straight ahead. Green fabric covered the floor. Lights hung overhead. If she wasn't mistaken, she was headed away from the arena, but going back the way she'd come only promised to land her in a face-off with the guard. She had to find a way into the arena!

But there was no way. The crowd's roar was no longer within earshot. She was about to head back when she saw a sign indicating that the passage to her right was a DRESSING ROOM. With some luck, it was a way back to the arena.

Silvie ran up the hall, ducked into the dressing room. Mirrors. Bright lights. Jewelry. One woman sat in a chair with her legs crossed, chewing on something as she worked on her nails.

Her eyes lifted. "Yes?"

"Sorry." Silvie closed the door, now on the brink of full-fledged panic. She had to get to him. Now, while he was still alive, assuming he *was* still alive! She didn't even know if he was in *this* arena.

A crowd's roar rose farther down the hall. Silvie blinked and looked back the way she'd come. The arena was ahead of her? She'd gone in a circle, perhaps.

Heart in her throat, she rushed toward a door topped by a sign reading STAGE. Without concern for her own safety, she flung the door open and barged into a room where several people sat about, watching square tubes with moving pictures on them of a woman singing. Piles of black boxes were identified in white letters: THE CRYING SHAME.

Silvie spun to her right and saw the same woman out on a stage, singing to a huge crowd partially hidden by long, black curtains. It took her only a moment to realize that she'd stumbled into a different arena; one reserved for song, not killing.

Without bothering to judge the expressions of those in the room, she backed out, slammed the door, whirled back the way she'd come, and sprinted down the hallway. She raced past the dressing room, along the lighted hall, and was about to duck back into the dark passageway alongside the arena when she saw a shaft of light to her right.

A break in the wall she'd missed coming the other direction.

Silvie ran up to a four-inch crack and peered into a huge, brightly lit arena with a dirt floor. There, on a platform in the center, stood Johnis. He held a knife in one hand, and his other was around an executioner's neck.

"Call him off, or I cut your throat where you stand!" he screamed.

"Johnis!"

Her own scream carried through the crack and echoed into the stadium. A thousand heads turned her way and, seeing nothing, immediately returned to the spectacle on the platform.

But Johnis understood.

"Silvie! Save yourself, Silvie."

"No, don't you dare say that! Let him free! He's not who you think he is!"

A pause.

"Tell them, Silvie," Johnis cried. "Tell them we're not the prisoners they think we are."

"We're not!" she screamed through the crack in the tall wall. "We're from the future. We've come here for the Books of History. It's all a mistake!"

There was another pause.

"Tell them we're related to the king," Johnis called.

The king? "We're related to the king."

"Take us to your supreme commander and let us sort this whole thing out!" Johnis yelled.

Silvie held her breath, eyes pressed up against the crack to see the crowd's response.

"Let me go!" the man in black growled.

His warriors moved as one, swarming for the platform.

"Johnis!"

nine

To say that the sound of Silvie's voice flooded Johnis with relief would be a gross understatement. He very nearly released the man and raced for the sound of it. She was here! She'd come to save him! But then he thought about the danger she was placing herself in, and his gratuitous relief turned to horror.

Their exchange didn't produce the kind of response he'd hoped for. He had a choice now: kill the man in his hands with a jerk of his knife and face them head-on, or take the chance that this interruption would stall the planned execution.

"You're cutting me," the executioner growled.

The warriors rushed.

"Johnis!"

A whistle blew shrilly. "Take him down, boys!"

Guards were pouring in through several doors along the wall. They'd found him. Regardless of what had really happened here, he was now at their mercy, which he doubted would be very liberal.

He released the man, let the knife fall to the platform, and lifted his hands in a show of surrender. "Run, Silvie! Save yourself! Find Darsal. Find Karas. Run!"

They fell on him with a tangle of sweaty arms and sharp curses. A pair of shiny silver shackles were clamped around his wrist and tightened. They hurried him from the building and shoved him into a Chevy with lights atop it, like the ones that had first given pursuit. Johnis slouched in the back, behind a cage that separated him from the pilot.

It took them only a few minutes to reach their prison and shuffle him into a plain white holding room with a table and chairs, all made of a white material like wood, but smoother and more uniform.

Johnis had never felt as lost as he did now.

"CALL ME SERGEANT CRAMSEY," THE OFFICER SAID, OFFER-ing his hand and sitting across the table from Johnis. "What would your name be?"

Seated here so helplessly, Johnis considered his options with growing pessimism. Silvie was out there, completely lost without him. They had no idea where Darsal or Karas were or how to get word to them. He was no longer sure if Las Vegas really was a

Horde city from the past or some kind of mix between human and Scab.

What he did know was that he felt sick for having lost Silvie. The forlorn sound of her voice crying for him from beyond the wall made his belly rise each time he thought about it, and he couldn't get her cry out of his mind. Tears threatened to overtake his eyes. He turned away from the man, unsure if he should tell him his name.

Then again, the only way to find Silvie, Darsal, or Karas was to make his whereabouts known. Johnis faced the Cramsey. "My name is Johnis."

"Last name?"

"Just Johnis. Johnis of Middle."

"Well, Johnis Middle, seems you've gotten yourself into a bit of trouble." He flipped through a report in his hands. "Reckless driving, speeding, stolen vehicle, disrupting the peace, attempted manslaughter . . . What the heck were you thinking, boy?"

"I was thinking they wanted to execute me."

"You expect me to believe that you raced into the Excalibur with real weapons and put a blade to a man's throat because you believed someone was after you?"

Johnis looked up at a thin glass box with moving pictures. Another amazing invention from the Histories. It was all far more than he could grasp.

"What is that?"

The officer looked at the glass box. "A Net screen. The Net, the news. I don't suppose you've ever seen the Net."

He frowned and shook his head. "No, I haven't."

A box on the man's waist burped, and he lifted it to his ear. He listened, eyes flittering to the Net, then Johnis. He lifted another instrument with multiple buttons and waved it at the glass box. The Net. The picture changed to a fuzzy one of a woman on a stage. The one behind held a knife to the other's neck. The picture grew larger.

Johnis jumped to his feet. "Silvie?" How was that possible? She was in the box, or an image of her was in the box.

Silvie was on a stage, holding a singer hostage, surrounded by a dozen panicked onlookers.

"You know her?" Cramsey asked. He pressed another button, and voices spoke from the box. Johnis watch in stunned amazement.

". . . moments ago an unidentified assailant rushed in from the side of the stage and took Mira Silver, lead singer of the band The Crying Shame, hostage at knife point . . . uh . . . honestly, this is quite unprecedented. The show was being aired live, Gene. What we're seeing is live. I repeat, we are live at the Excalibur in Las Vegas, where an unknown . . ."

The sound went dead.

"You know her?"

"It's Silvie! Yes, yes, I know her." Johnis scrambled over to the Net and slapped its side. "What happened to her voice?"

As if by magic, the box spoke again, and he jumped back. Silvie was screaming now.

"You hear me? Not a hundred yards from here they took my

lover, Johnis of Middle. He was guilty of nothing but following the directives of the Roush to find the lost Books of History, three of which are in this world."

She paused, panting, eyes wide. Her strained voiced came again, wavering in fear this time.

"I realize these are extreme measures, but . . ." A close-up showed her face, tears leaking from the corners of her eyes. "You give me no choice. I know you have him. Give me Johnis, and I will let this one live."

Johnis spun to Cramsey, who was eyeing him carefully. "You have to take me to her. She'll kill her!"

No sign of concern crossed the man's face.

Johnis plopped in a chair. "Then her blood is on your head. But don't tell me I didn't warn you. Believe me when I say I know Silvie. She'd gut a hundred Scabs before one could put a blade in her. This will *not* end well!"

He knew that he was overly expressive, but his eagerness to undo what he had drawn Silvie into was overpowering.

Silvie was talking again. "I mean no harm. But don't think we can be discounted easily. My name is Silvie of Southern, and I will not rest until I have Johnis of Middle in my arms again." She caught herself, then pushed forward.

"We did not come here to cause any trouble but to save humanity before the Dark One enslaves us all. You must set him free. I beg you!"

Johnis slammed his fist on the table. "Free us!"

"Settle down, boy. If I free you now, it'll be right into the cus-tody of the fruit farm. You want that?"

"As long as I'm with her"—he stood and shoved his finger at the box—"you may put me wherever you wish."

"Then talk her in. Tell her this is all a mistake. We can sort out the 'Books of History' business later."

Silvie was pulling her hostage backward now, her knife pressed tight against her skin. Mira Silver looked like she'd swallowed a lemon, but she wasn't a hysterical mess like others around her. The picture jerked to show the audience who'd come to watch The Crying Shame perform.

They both walked off stage, disappeared behind the curtain.

Johnis stared after Silvie, wishing her to reappear. The announcer came back on, explaining what she'd already said. Cramsey silenced the box.

"If I can see her on this box, can she see me?" Johnis demanded.

"I don't know what you two are up to, but you've just bought yourself more trouble than you can imagine."

"I have to talk to her! Can she see me?"

The door opened and another officer walked in. He glanced up at the muted Net. "You see that?"

"Yes, sir. I did."

"She has Mira Silver held up in her dressing room. The mayor wants the casino evacuated. This thing's playing on every channel on the Web." The man glanced at Johnis. "Get anywhere with him?"

"They're partners, sir. He wants to talk to her."

The superior frowned. "Mira Silver, of all people. She might as well have taken the president hostage. This doesn't look good, Jake. The news is reporting that this one made a fool of our boys on the south side."

"Then you must let me talk to her now," Johnis said. "Before she makes fools of even more of your men."

"She ain't making fools of my men. Because when she comes out, we're going to put her down."

ten

Silvie paced before the mirror, absently twirling both bone-handled knives by her side. The soft whirring sound was a faint reminder of her place in another world where she was Silvie of Southern, chosen from one thousand young fighters to lead. A hero, skilled with knives and, above all, Forest Guard in the service of Thomas of Hunter.

Yet here . . .

Here she was a fugitive who'd taken a singer hostage in desperation, lost from Johnis, whom she loved. Here she was a mouse among elephants, a spider in the lake, an emotional wreck with a captive who was far more at ease than she.

"You know you're toast down here," Mira said.

"Hush! I'm trying to think."

Silvie looked at the woman studying her with an even gaze. Mira looked to be in her early twenties, a dancer who could sing as well as anyone Silvie had heard in the forests. The dance moves she'd seen the performer execute were more rigid and precise than those the dancers in Southern preferred, but even in the few moments she watched through the curtains before her attack, Silvie could see that she was a master of her craft.

"I can help you think," Mira said.

"You take me for a fool who needs the help of an artist?"

"The thought had crossed my mind. Why are you dressed up like that?"

"I'm a fighter, not a dancer who prances about in a short skirt."

"A fighter who's looking for the lost Books of History," Mira said. "Right, I'd forgotten. Problem is"—she stood, against Silvie's orders, and started for the door—"no one here has any clue who this Johnis is or what the Books of History are. You're wasting your time."

"Where are you going?"

"I'm leaving."

Silvie sprang for the singer, dragged her back to her seat, and pushed her down. "I told you I'd bind you if you tried to get away."

"Ouch. Not so hard!"

"I told you: I'm a warrior not a dancer. Breaking your neck is something I could do with one hand. Don't test me."

Silvie snatched up a tubular contraption with a cord attached and wound the cord around Mira's wrists, then tied it off. "Stay!"

"Tell me about these little white, fuzzy creatures again."

She'd made the mistake of telling Mira about the Roush and the Shataiki in an attempt to gain her understanding. Her explanations had gained her only the kind of sympathy you might have for an idiot.

"The Roush," she said.

"Sounds like fun. But here, in the real world, there are no little fuzzy bats. You just have to accept that, Silvie. No Roush are coming to your rescue. Outside this room, they'll shoot you dead for what you've done. I may be your prisoner for the moment, honey, but trust me, I'm the only one around here who can help you."

"And how would you do that?" Silvie snapped. She felt like dropping to her knees and sobbing, right there in front of Mira. "They took Johnis!"

"You're in love with Johnis, and I can appreciate that. But you don't take a girl hostage for love. Not if you want to stay out of prison—and especially not a famous pop star!"

"He's not just the one I love! He's the chosen one, singled out by the Roush and by Elyon himself to recover the seven lost Books of History before the—"

"—Dark One enslaves the world," Mira finished. "Yes, I know. But you have to get a grip here, honey. They're going to crucify you out there."

"But you believe me, right?"

"Well, yes, I can help you."

"Fine. Tell me."

"For starters, you have to start communicating," Mira said.

"How?"

"There's no phone in here; you'll have to pass them a note. Tell them there's been a misunderstanding. Get some dialogue going. Turn on the Net and find out what they're saying on the news. Get a feeling for what you've done."

"What's a Net?"

Mira grinned. "Come on, don't do that."

"I'm not doing anything. Where Johnis and I come from, there is no such thing that I've heard of."

"Okay, fine. See that black box over there?" She motioned to a glass box with her chin. "You push the little green button below the screen."

Silvie walked up to the Net, keeping Mira in her peripheral view in the event this was a ploy. "How do I know this isn't some fancy weapon that will finish me off?"

"Let me turn it on, if you doubt me."

"No."

"Then push the button! It won't bite."

Silvie pushed the button. A picture filled the glass surface, and she jumped back, ready to defend against any attack.

"See, no harm. Now hand me the remote." Mira nodded at a black object on the counter. She handed the remote to her prisoner, who pressed another button.

The picture on the Net changed. A woman with dark hair was talking earnestly about what they were calling "the Mira Silver kidnapping." But what amazed Silvie even more was the smaller box to the woman's right on which the events of the kidnapping were being played out nearly identically as . . .

No, it was an actual replay of what had happened. Silvie watched herself behind Mira, crying out for all to hear her demands.

"That's us!"

"You really don't know what the Net is?"

The picture suddenly changed. An image of a prison filled the glass. Vertical bars behind which stood a man.

Johnis.

"It's . . ." Silvie took a step back, stunned at the sight. "It's Johnis." They had Johnis in a prison! "I told you!" she cried.

Mira didn't reply.

The picture of him grew until his whole face filled the screen, showing clearly his dusty cheeks, his small, smudged nose. A cut on his lip—from his fight in the arena or from torture, she couldn't tell.

Then his voice, as clear as if he were standing in that very room, was talking to her.

"Silvie . . ." He paused, glancing to his right. "I've made a deal to tell them everything I know in exchange for going on the Net, so I hope you can hear me. I saw what you did, Silvie. And I'm moved that you would put yourself in such danger for me. For us. None of them seem to have a clue about the Books of History, but I believe that when this is all over, you will be remembered as much as . . ."

He glanced off to his right and snapped at whoever was watching him on the other end. "I'll say what I want; that is what we agreed to!"

He returned his attention to the screen. "Forgive me. You will be remembered for your bravery. The Roush are watching, Silvie. History itself is watching. For all we know, Thomas Hunter is watching."

"Who?" Mira asked.

"Thomas Hunter," Silvie said absently. "Supreme commander of the Forest Guard."

"*The* Thomas Hunter?"

Silvie ignored her. She moved closer to the Net.

Johnis took a deep breath. "They've shown me the forces gathered around the Excalibur, Silvie. Chevys too many to count. 'Police cars,' they're called. Officers armed with the fire sticks. Shotguns. The only hope we have is for you to join me here, where they've given me their word they will listen to our story."

She could read the pleading lines in his face, no sign that he was saying one thing while sending a different signal.

"If they were the Horde, I would tell you to fight your way out or die trying. But I don't think they are. Stupid, yes, but not wrong in what they are doing. And Darsal, Karas, if you see me or hear me, please come to our aide. Our lives may now depend on you."

He paused again, then spoke softly.

"I love you, Silvie."

"And I love you, Johnis," she said. Tears flooded her eyes. "I love you!"

The picture changed to the announcer again. "Well, there you have it, ladies and gentleman, in this most unusual . . ."

Silvie spun to her prisoner. "Take me to him! Make me your captive and protect me. Just take me to him. It's all I ask."

A faint smile crossed Mira's mouth. "You love him."

"I do! More than you know!"

"Just like that?"

"Don't you see? He's used this invention of yours to call out to Darsal and Karas. You said this will be seen by many."

"By half the world. And you'll be lucky if they don't lock you up."

"Without Darsal and Karas our mission is lost. If they're alive, I hope they will have seen us on this Net of yours. Take me to Johnis."

Mira didn't jump and run for the door as any weaker captive might have. She studied Silvie with what could be interpreted as empathy. Mira was a true romantic at heart, likely what inspired her performances on stage.

"You're in a predicament, honey."

eleven

She stood in the main library, eyes fixed on the large screen that replayed the events half a world away in Las Vegas, Nevada. So then, he was right. They weren't the quiet type, these chosen ones.

Desire sliced through her chest. It had begun, hadn't it? The fate of so many after so much time rested in what so few would do in the next few days.

A voice spoke behind her, soft but as definite as a hammer to the forehead. "Bring them to me."

She turned casually. He was dressed in the black cape.

"The books and Johnis, as planned."

"I know my role," she snapped. "Concern yourself with yours."

"Yet you're still here."

She strode toward the door.

"Remember, Mirandaaaaa . . ." He let her name fade in a breath. She stopped at the door but did not face him. "If you fail me now, you'll be dead before they are. I don't need you."

She resisted the temptation to explain to him how wrong he was. Useless. In the seven years they'd known each other, she'd never known him to make even the slightest miscalculation in his judgment. Except this one.

"Godspeed," he said.

Oh, the irony of it all.

twelve

Johnis and Silvie sat in the same jail cell, waiting for the authorities to make some sense of the psychiatrist's findings, though Silvie couldn't imagine that the results of such an absurd test could have any bearing on guilt or innocence.

The fact was, they were both guilty of all of it. They had stolen a Chevy. Fled the police. Driven recklessly. Caused a disturbance at the Excalibur. Kidnapped a world-famous pop star. And lived to tell.

This morning their faces had filled the Net screen nonstop. It was now afternoon, and already the attention had shifted to other interests, which was fine by them.

"The doctor's a charlatan!" Johnis snapped, walking the length of their ten-by-ten cell. They'd been permitted to share the cell, as negotiated by Johnis as part of Silvie's surrender.

"Agreed," Silvie said.

"Boxes and triangles and . . . bah!" Johnis dismissed the examination with a flip of his wrist.

"So we just wait?"

"What else?"

Johnis had explained his reasoning. Silvie'd been right: he'd used the Net to reach Darsal and Karas. But neither had.

"For all we know, they're dead," Silvie said.

"Then so are we."

"You don't believe that. We've been in worse predicaments. In Teeleh's lair. In the Horde city."

"Did Teeleh have shotguns? Or flying cars? Do you see Roush or the Guard rushing to our defense? We don't even have the books we came with. The authorities took everything!"

Their battle dress and the books had been confiscated, along with their knives. They now wore the white-and-brown striped slacks and smocks common among all prisoners here.

Silvie walked up to the bars and gripped them with both hands. "We have each other."

No response from Johnis. When she turned, she saw that he was nibbling on his fingernail, lost in thought.

"You forget so quickly?" Silvie demanded.

"What? What—no. Yes, we have each other. It'll have to do."

"Have to do? You threw yourself in a cage for your mother. You nearly gave up your life for Karas. But for me it'll just 'have to do'?"

"No." He gripped his hair and paced. "That's not what I meant."

The poor boy was reeling; she had no business testing his

love at such a time. But the urge to act on her emotions felt irresistible.

She closed her eyes and bit her lip. *You're as frantic as he, Silvie. Control yourself.* Then she felt his hand on her shoulder, pulling her close. Warmth filled her belly. He'd seen her disappointment and rushed to her side.

Johnis held her in his arms and spoke quickly into her ear. "I'm stronger and faster than I was before. They can't know, but there's a chance we may be superior to them." A few breaths in her ear, enough for her to realize that his embrace was for communication rather than consolation.

"Have you noticed?"

She swallowed. "Yes, but not strong enough to take them on."

"But fast enough."

"You said yourself, we don't stand a chance!"

No response. His suggestion was one of raw desperation.

A bang on the bars startled them. "Okay, love birds, I've got good news for both of you."

The guard they called "Guns" grinned at them from beyond the cage. He slapped his palm with a black stick. "The Kook says you two are not. Kooks, that is. You're as sane as I am, which, to be perfectly honest with you, ain't saying a lot."

He twitched, and nearby another guard chuckled.

"Now the bad news. Seeing as you aren't headed to the fruit farm right quick, they're going to ship you down to the main jail, where they send the hard cases." His twisted grin said it all. "If I was you, I'd think twice about this 'we're from another world' routine, 'we got no money, no kin, no guilt' junk, and start making sense."

"Back off, Guns." The detective who'd struck the deal with Johnis spoke from down the hall—Cramsey. "Open it up."

Guns sprang the latch, pulled the gate wide. Cramsey stepped up and stared at them. "Seems you have attracted attention from a friend in high places. Mira has suddenly decided to drop all kidnapping charges, and the DA has inexplicably dropped the others, paid off, if you ask me. They've made arrangements to release you. But if I see your face again, it won't go easy, you hear? And drop the stupid act. It never works." Then to someone down the hall, "They're all yours."

A woman walked into view, and Silvie felt her muscles tense. She was slightly older, perhaps in her early twenties, though she carried herself like someone who'd been around much longer.

Short, well formed, dressed in the blue trousers so many here wore, wearing shoes with high heels, which was also customary in this world, no matter how crippling they seemed. Her blouse was black; she wore a silver necklace with a large onyx pendent in the shape of a circle. Long, brown hair. Green eyes staring at them in wonder. Stern. Silvie knew this woman. She couldn't place her name, but they'd met.

For a moment neither spoke. Then the woman dipped her head enough to acknowledge a bond. "Hello, Silvie." Beat. "It's been a long time."

Johnis took a step forward. "Karas?"

"Hello, Johnis."

thirteen

As soon as Johnis said it, Silvie knew he was right. This was either Karas or her twin sister, ten years older!

"What . . . how?"

"Not here," the woman said. "I have transportation waiting." Then to Cramsey, a bite in her voice, "Bring them!"

"Of course, Ms. Longford."

Silvie exchanged a wide-eyed glance with Johnis and followed. The woman walked with clean steps, elegant despite the tall shoes, as those with privilege and authority walked.

"We came through after she did," Johnis mumbled to himself. "So long?"

Karas looked over her shoulder. "Not now."

They followed her through the station, out into the open, to a long, black car that waited at the curb. An attendant opened the door for them.

"Climb in. After you."

Silvie and Johnis slid into a richly upholstered chamber with two facing leather benches. Karas took the seat opposite them and waited for the attendant to close the door.

Silence engulfed them. Karas stared for a long time, still not smiling, and for a moment Silvie felt more alarm than relief. Then the girl's eyes flooded with tears that spilled down her cheeks. She lowered her head into one hand and sobbed quietly.

The car began to move.

"Is it really you?" Johnis asked.

Karas lifted her face and beamed through her tears. "Yes, it's me, you scrapper!" She fell forward on her knees and threw her arms around their necks, pulling them into an embrace that threatened to choke them.

"You have no idea how long I've waited for this day! Elyon, dear Elyon, I knew it would come!"

The last of Silvie's lingering doubts fell like loosed chains. Karas slid back on the leather seat and wiped her cheek with her fingers. "I could hardly believe my eyes when I played the tape last night. I'm sorry; I would have come sooner, but I was at a concert in Amsterdam. How long have you been here?"

Johnis still looked like he'd been kicked by a mule. "Two days?"

"Two days!" Karas cried, then cackled with laughter. "So, then, you think the world's turned inside out."

Johnis swallowed. "It has."

"What do you know? You've seen the lights, the cars? Well, obviously the cars—you're riding in one. And you were both on the Net. A bit overwhelming, I'm sure."

"I've mastered the Chevy," Johnis said.

She smiled wide. "So I heard." She began to cry again. "I *knew* I hadn't lost my mind. For ten years I've had to wonder if it really was all a dream. The forests, the Horde, bathing in the lakes. All of it! But it's true, isn't it?"

"True?" Silvie looked out the window. "The question is, is *this* true?" She turned back to Karas. "Are *you* true? I mean, you're real, of course, but . . . look at you!"

"You're a woman," Johnis said. There was more than a hint of wonder in his voice, and Silvie wasn't sure she wanted to share his enthusiasm. She wasn't just a woman; she was a beautiful woman of significant wealth and influence.

"How old are you?" she asked.

"Twenty-one. But I tell them all I'm twenty-four—it suits my place as an entertainment manager in this world. They have a hard enough time believing that someone in her midtwenties could have accomplished what I have. If they knew how young I really was, they'd dig even deeper than they do."

"Younger?" Johnis said. "You look old enough."

"There's so much to cover," Karas said, smiling through her tears. "I've hoped for this day for as long as I can remember. Nothing else matters. I've done it all hoping that one day I would find you. I just had no idea you would both be so . . . young still."

"We're sixteen," Silvie said. "Is that so young?"

"No. Although in the United States, sixteen isn't the age of marrying and waging war." She stopped, clearly overwhelmed. "It's so . . . refreshing to talk to someone besides my therapist about Other Earth. Did you know that Thomas Hunter was once a great hero here?"

"So, he *was* here?" Johnis asked in amazement. "This is the place from his dreams?"

"From what I can tell, Other Earth—that's what I call it—is the far future of Earth. At some point in the future here, this Earth is destroyed and everything starts over. Thomas Hunter found a way from this reality into that future."

"Then . . . can we?"

"I don't know. Not with only one book. Maybe with all four."

Karas reached into a box on the seat beside her. She carefully lifted out the brown book Johnis had used and then the green one that had brought Silvie through.

"I have the black one," Karas said, brushing her fingers over the covers as if they held the essence of her very life—which they might well.

"And Darsal?" Johnis asked.

She lifted her eyes. "I don't know."

"Then we have to find her."

Once again, tears filled Karas's eyes. "I'm sorry. I don't mean to be such a sap. So much has transpired in these last ten years. It's so good to see you."

It occurred to Silvie that, for her and Johnis, only two days had passed since they'd left their world to find themselves here, in the Histories. But Karas had survived here, in this hell, for more than ten years. She wouldn't have guessed such a thing was possible, especially for a ten-year-old. The poor girl had suffered enormously.

"So much has happened." Karas looked at the two Books of History on her lap. "I hardly know where to start."

"Tell us everything," Johnis said.

"In good time, my friend. In good time." The car slowed, then stopped. "We're here."

They exited the car behind Karas and stood before a long, tubular vehicle with fixed wings. It was one of the birds they'd seen fly overhead. Two large mouths were attached to the body, and from these mouths came a high-pitched whine that made Silvie step back.

"Ever dreamed of flying?" Karas asked, beaming.

The idea startled Silvie. "In the sky?"

"Yes, in the sky. Like a bird."

"In that thing?"

"In that thing."

Johnis's eyes were round. "Is it a Chevy?"

"No, it's a Citation 20. And it's faster than a Chevy."

"Fantastic," Johnis said.

FLYING OVER EARTH AT TWENTY THOUSAND FEET WAS AN experience that made Silvie forget all the disadvantages the Histories had presented up to this point. Neither she nor Johnis seemed to be able to hide their grins, peering out through the round windows.

"One of these contraptions would end the war with the Horde," Johnis said.

"How so?"

"You could fly over them and drop boulders without any fear of being cut down."

"Trust me, Johnis, you could drop more than rocks to end the war with the Horde," Karas said. "But you wouldn't want to kill so many others like me."

She still has a soft spot in her heart for the Scabs, Silvie thought, returning her attention to the clouds beneath the airplane.

They talked about the short past they'd shared, beginning with the details of Karas's rescue from the Horde City. She wanted to rehearse every detail from her memory, just to be sure she'd remembered it all as it really had happened.

Then she quickly told them about her journey through the desert with Darsal. Meeting Alucard in the Black Forest. Their escape into the cover of this world, a virtual reality that could be accessed by touching any of the seven books with blood—which is what Billos had done when he'd gone renegade on them.

"I've done it a dozen times since," Karas said. "It's like walking into a simulation of this reality. Paradise, every time. The point is, Paradise, Colorado, is real. I've been there."

"And?"

"Nothing."

"But that was before we arrived with our two books," Johnis said. "Until our books entered this reality, there were only two books here: yours and Darsal's."

Which begged the question Silvie voiced. "No sign of Darsal at all?"

Karas stared out at the blue sky. "I've searched, trust me. When all of my efforts failed, I followed this path." She motioned to the jet, meaning her life as a manager. "If I couldn't find you two or Darsal, I wanted to make sure you could find me. So I've used what skills I have to make myself highly visible. As it turned out, you managed more visibility in one day than I have in five years."

An exaggeration, but point well made.

"Darsal's never contacted me. Which means she's either dead . . ."

"Or hasn't come through yet," Johnis finished. "For all we know, she may not come through for another ten years."

"Correct. As is the case with Alucard."

"So . . . if Darsal hasn't come through yet, only our three books have come through thus far. The other three books hidden here may not even be visible yet?"

"Possibly," Karas said. "If Darsal did come through, she's clearly run into trouble, or she would have contacted me. Whoever has her book might know about me. If so, they're probably waiting for you two to surface before they expose themselves and go for all of our books at once."

The soft rush of air from the engines outside filled the cabin.

"No sign of that beast?" Silvie asked. "Alucard?"

"Signs?" Karas frowned. "Everywhere you look. What is Alucard but raw wickedness in the form of Shataiki? It's everywhere. But no, I haven't seen any Shataiki floating through the night sky."

"Then let's keep out fingers crossed," Johnis said. "With any luck, we find the seven books before he comes through."

"We have to assume he's through as well, biding his time, waiting for you two to show up," Karas said. "And we might be wise to assume the worst."

Johnis frowned. "That he has Darsal's book. That he's killed her and is biding his time."

It seemed rather pessimistic to Silvie, and she made as much clear.

"Maybe," Karas said. "But I've run through every possible scenario a thousand times over the years, and I assure you, we'd better be prepared for the worst, because I have a nasty feeling your little stunt on the Net set into motion much more than you bargained for."

Karas's speculation put a bit of a damper on the flight, but it was quickly overcome by the jet's sudden descent and frightening maneuvering over a sprawling compound of white buildings and small bodies of blue water she called "swimming pools."

They were flying over her house. A small town by all measures, nestled in the hills above the city of angels: Los Angeles. They would set down on a private airstrip, freshen up, and change into clothing more suitable than the prison smocks they currently wore.

All this according to Karas, who gave them a running commentary. Silvie wasn't entirely sure what it all meant, but she took it in wearing the same look of dumb wonder that was plastered on Johnis's face. Though she suspected by the comments he kept making that he was under the illusion he understood perfectly.

They landed, exited the airplane, and took a car to the main house. More accurately, the mansion. Towering white columns supported a huge ceiling that arched over the main atrium. Several servants greeted them, one at the front door, one in the kitchen, another near the pool area that overlooked the city below.

It was all a bit much for Silvie, but Karas glided around on her bare feet as naturally as a sparrow who'd come home to her nest.

They would eat at seven, she informed the cook—after the concert. Lobster and aged Kobe beef for the guests tonight; let's show them what the Histories have to offer.

She effortlessly ran through a stack of notes handed to her by a secretary wearing jeans and named Rick Cumberland, directing the man on a number of urgent issues, as though doing so were as natural as eating a meal.

The butler showed Sylvie and Johnis to two bedrooms where he'd laid out several outfits of new clothing as instructed by Karas. They reconvened on the patio—Johnis dressed in loose-fitting jeans with a black T-shirt, and Silvie in a black skirt with a white, sleeveless top. Johnis opted for boots. Silvie, sandals.

Karas looked them over and nodded her approval. "Not bad. You'll fit right in."

"Fit right in where?"

"I'm introducing one of my singers, Tony Montana, at a concert in the Rose Bowl. Something I foolishly agreed to do when a client wins in their respective categories at all major awards shows, which Tony did at the 12th annual VH2 Awards last week. We'll leave for the Rose Bowl by helicopter in an hour."

"A bowl?"

"A little larger than a bowl, actually," Karas laughed.

fourteen

They sat around a round table, staring out at the city, with a light breeze in their hair, the orange sun dipping to their sides, and delicacies at their fingertips. Karas, known here as Kara Longford, told them her story, and hearing it all, Silvie couldn't stop shaking her head in wonder.

She'd arrived in Nevada, as they had—why Nevada, she didn't know. A ten-year-old girl, she was lost and terrified on a highway that led to the big city of lights. She tried to be brave those first few days but couldn't stop crying.

There was no shortage of people willing to help a little girl who needed food and money, but none of them had any answers for her, and they all looked at her as if she'd lost her mind when she asked about the Horde or the Shataiki.

She took up with an old man who lived under a bridge after a week of wandering. "Scotty," he called himself, after a character from an old show called *Star Trek*. Unlike others, Scotty's eye lit up when she talked about the Horde and the Books of History. And thank Elyon, because if not for Scotty, she would have undoubtedly been committed to the fruit farm, a colloquial expression for a mental hospital.

Outside of Scotty's protective oversight, she became known as the little girl who would take your head off at the drop of a hat. A mental case, to be sure.

It wasn't until she went through therapy years later that she figured out what was wrong those first few months. Her emotions had been affected by the transition between the future and the Histories.

"Really?" Johnis shot Silvie a look of understanding.

"You've noticed?" Karas asked.

"I think it's what got us into trouble with the Chevy," Silvie said. "Johnis practically went berserk."

Johnis grinned sheepishly. "It did bring a few of our feelings to the surface."

Karas lifted an eyebrow, looking from one to the other. "Don't worry; it passes."

"We're not looking for it to pass," Silvie said. "Ever."

"I'm not talking about the love you've vowed for each other on the Net. I'm talking about the raw emotions caused by the transition between worlds. And your thinking feels a bit sluggish, right?"

"Careless. A little stupid, maybe. We're stuck with this?"

"No. The fact is, your mind isn't sluggish. Just the opposite. Your intelligence is well advanced over the average person here, so far advanced that it's struggling to compensate for the surge of emotional responses filtering through your mind. At least that's my best guess after the countless rounds of psychological testing I subjected myself to in an attempt to understand."

"But you're saying our minds will compensate soon enough?"

Karas nodded. "Have you noticed anything else?"

"Speed," Johnis said.

"Bingo . . . Sorry, just an expression. Our reflexes and strength are superior to the humans from the Histories. Not by much, but enough to pull out a few tricks now and then. Still, it's nothing compared to the advantage your minds will give you."

Karas went on to retrace her history here: How she'd soon begun compensating for her heightened emotions with a superior intellect. How she'd started using that intellect when she was thirteen to win small bets involving certain mathematical problems, then graduated to more complex problems. "Sleight of mind," she called it. Soon she was headlining as a child prodigy in her own stage show.

She studied on her own during the day and began building a small fortune performing in the evening. By the time she was fifteen, she'd exhausted the requirements of primary education and enrolled in a Web-based university program, studying entertainment business management with a secondary emphasis in language and history.

All the while, she had used every possible avenue to search for them. For Darsal. For Alucard. All to no avail.

Her plan was well formed even then. She would learn everything she could about history, never relenting in her ambition to find the companion books to the black Book of History in her possession. She would learn as many languages as she thought necessary to assist her in a global search for her friends and the books. And she would launch a career using her advanced intelligence to give her the broad access and exposure needed for her search. Rather than entertain, she would *manage* entertainers, creating both wealth and exposure through high-profile artists.

Most importantly, she would appear with her artists onstage frequently, so that she, too, would become world renowned. If Alucard was out there, and she had to assume that he was, she had to be visible enough worldwide to attract the attention of Johnis, Silvie, and Darsal before he got to them.

"So you've succeeded in all of this," Silvie said, stating what seemed to be obvious. "Well enough to spring us from jail."

"That was harder than you might guess. Fortunately, I manage the girl you kidnapped, and I'm very tight with the authorities in Las Vegas. The chief of police owes me a dozen favors. At this moment I manage fifteen of the top billing acts in the world through Global Entertainment Network, GEN."

"You'd think the warriors would own the wealth, not the artists," Johnis said, looking around the lavish setting.

She laughed. "There's plenty of money in war—always has

been, always will be. But humans will pay as much for their thrills as they will for their security. Was it any different in the forests? The first thing I noticed in Middle were the nightly celebrations."

"Like I've always said"—Johnis winked at Silvie—"'a poet is worth two fighters.' Just ask Elyon."

"There's more than one way to carve a poem," Silvie said, twirling her knife from a fold in her blouse. She slammed it into the table they were seated around.

"Nice," Karas said. "That is a ten-thousand-dollar slab of sandalwood from Indonesia you just defaced."

"The knife is from the future and will fetch you ten times that," Silvie responded.

"Touché."

"So, just how much wealth have you managed to acquire in your time here?"

"Enough to own a small country if I so choose. You once told me about the game Thomas Hunter taught you to play with the Horde ball."

"It was how we were first chosen," Silvie said.

"It's a very big game here; they call it 'football.' I own two teams. With your speed, you could both become huge stars here."

Johnis spit to one side. "Doesn't interest me."

"Please, we're not in a jungle here," Silvie chided. "Mind your manners."

"Sorry."

Karas let out a short giggle. "Brings back memories."

"Yes, sorry." He took a deep breath. "There is something I was wondering if you might help me with. Assuming it's not too much trouble. I don't want to presume upon your wealth, but—"

"Enough," Karas said. "My wealth is your wealth. What is it?"

He spoke before she'd fully finished. "A Chevy." His eyes shone like the stars. "A red Chevy."

Karas smiled. "Like the beauty you stole in Nevada? The sweet racer with the cherry paint job and souped-up engine that you tore up Las Vegas with?"

"Yes. That Chevy."

"Not a problem, my friend. I bought it as part of your get-out-of-jail package. Cost me twice what the owner had in it, but I paid every dime gladly. One day that car will go down in history. The Chevy that Johnis of Middle, world-renowned driver, first learned to drive in." She stood. "In the meantime, I have something else for you. Wait here."

Karas returned a minute later, gripping a wooden box in both hands. She set it gingerly on the table, opened it, and withdrew the black Book of History she'd harbored for all these years.

She set it next to theirs. The three books sat side by side: one brown, one green, one black.

Johnis stood and walked around the table. "We have to protect these at any cost."

"I've spared no expense doing so. I'll show you the vault before we leave. No one can know. For all we know, he's watching us at this very moment."

"Alucard?" Silvie glanced at the perimeter.

"From a satellite in the sky," Karas said. "From the stars. Unlikely, but we have to be careful."

"Then let's take a new vow," Johnis said. He dropped to one knee and placed his right hand on the black book. "To never stray from our task of finding the seven before the Dark One does."

Silvie placed her cool palm over his knuckles. Then Karas, with wide eyes, joined the ranks of the chosen.

"To never stray from our task of finding the seven before the Dark One does," they said together.

"Though far from home, to remain home in our hearts, never to betray each other or the books."

Their eyes met in solemn intent. "Though far from home, to remain home in our hearts, never to betray each other or the books."

"Until the books are found or we die."

"Until the books are found or we die."

THE HELICOPTER REMINDED SILVIE OF A FLYING BEETLE, complete with beating wings and bug eyes, and it took a little encouragement from Karas to get her inside the apparatus.

The Rose Bowl, as it turned out, was a large stadium filled to capacity with onlookers who'd come to see Tony Montana perform. Karas instructed the pilot to hover over the scene while she explained how it all worked. The lights, the long lines of cars, the sound system.

"Absurd," Silvie scoffed.

Johnis turned from the glass door. "How is this any different than our own celebrations?"

"To hear a few people sing?"

"Your mind is too consumed with war, Silvie! Our own gathering isn't so different. And the gatherings of the legends! In the end we were made to celebrate; isn't that part of the Great Romance?"

In those terms he was right, of course. But she didn't waste the opportunity to refocus his mind. "Love, my dear," she said, winking. "The Great Romance is all about love."

His face blushed. "Yes. Love."

His entire demeanor seemed to have shifted a little off center since coming to the Histories, she thought. He was more excitable than stoic.

"You think this is something? You should see Agnew take the stage when I can convince them to come out of hiding. Their concerts sell out in hours, regardless of the venue," Karas said into her mouthpiece. "Take her down, Peter."

They landed behind the stage and were ushered in by a contingent of black-suited guards awaiting their arrival. Karas acknowledged each with a nod, a shake of the hand, a smile. By all that Silvie could see, Karas was widely admired here.

They hurried into a "green" room, which was actually a dirty white room under the stadium. Tony Montana was a slight man, dressed in a black shirt and a white headband. His jeans were torn, perhaps to give the illusion that he'd just come from battle, although Silvie knew nothing could be farther from the truth. The way handlers busied themselves around him, offering him drinks and delicacies, she doubted he'd ever lifted a shovel, much less a sword.

Any doubts she had about this man the throngs had come to adore fell to the side when he turned and looked at her. His eyes were a bright blue, a complete contrast to his dark skin and black, tangled hair. He studied her with interest, simultaneously intense and innocent. But more than all of this, his face, the pouting shape of his lips, the small nose, the baby-smooth skin. Apart from his blue eyes, Tony Montana reminded her very much of Johnis.

Karas took Silvie's arm. "You see it too?"

"He looks . . ." Silvie paused, not sure she should make the comparison.

"Like Johnis," Karas said. "If I ever allow myself to fall in love, it will be with this man." She stepped up to the rock star. "Hello, Tony. I would like you to meet the two most important people in the world to me."

He kissed her cheek. "And here I thought I occupied one of those places." To Silvie, dipping his head, "A pleasure."

Tony Montana made polite conversation, but as Johnis gained confidence, they began prying with questions that seemed to genuinely engage each other. Soon they were in a deep discussion about poetry and beauty and love and all things creative.

An attendant with an earpiece approached them from a side door. "Sixty seconds, Kara."

Karas nodded. "You ready, Tony?"

"Always, my dear."

She nodded to the attendant. "Take my friends to the press box. I'll join you in a few . . ."

She stopped, slipped a thin black card from her jeans, and stared at a red light that blinked on one end.

"Kara?" Tony touched her elbow. "Everything okay?"

She blinked. Slid the card back into her pocket. "Fine." But her face had paled. "I'll meet you in the box."

They watched from the press box as Karas took the stage to the sound of cheering cries that suggested *she* was the star they'd come to see, Silvie thought. It was hard to imagine that this frail-looking woman had been a little girl trapped in Witch's dungeon only a week earlier, at least from her perspective. Yet here she was, acknowledging the roaring approval of a hundred thousand fans in the Histories.

Then Karas introduced Tony Montana, and the stadium trembled with pounding hands and feet. The lights went out, smoke rose on the stage, a single drum began to thump, and Silvie held her breath.

She wasn't ready for the thunder that followed. Lightening stuttered on the stage, blinding them. The drums pounded. Silvie grabbed Johnis's arm.

Tony leaped higher than seemed natural, his legs twisted to one side, and when his feet landed, the guitars roared. Music, the screaming variety she'd heard earlier, shook the stadium.

"Fantastic!"

She turned to see Johnis grinning from ear to ear. His delight was infectious. She had to agree: the sound of music from the Histories was, indeed, fantastic.

"Like it?"

Karas had come up behind them.

"Yes."

"Good. We have to go."

The black card, Silvie thought. *There's a problem.*

"What's wrong?" Johnis asked.

"I just talked to Rick. There's a woman at the house who refuses to give her name. We need to see her immediately."

"Why?"

"Because she claims to have a blue book with her. The blue Book of History."

fifteen

Karas walked with a quick, tense step. Silvie had watched her address a hundred thousand screaming fans as casually as a mother addressing her children before sending them off to bed. But news of one woman who claimed to have the fourth Book of History in her possession was enough to betray her true compass. Whatever others thought of Kara Longford's interests in entertainment here on Earth, in truth her heart teetered on the balances of good and evil in a world far, far away.

She flung the front door to her house wide before the butler had a chance to open it. "Where?"

"She's waiting in the atrium, my lady." He bowed.

Karas stepped out of her shoes and moved over the marble floor in her bare feet, followed closely by Johnis and Silvie.

The woman who refused to give her name stood on the patio next to the lighted pool, her back to them. The night horizon glimmered with a million city lights. A stiff breeze whipped at the guest's loose slacks and blue blouse. Her long, black hair flowed on the wind. Silvie could only think of one name: Darsal.

They stopped ten feet from the woman, silent in the night.

"May we help you?" Karas asked.

Their guest turned and stared at them. All hope that this woman might be Darsal vanished. The resemblance went no further than her dark hair and height. No scar. Cheekbones too high. Lips thinner. Arms thin, not muscular from battle.

"Kara Longford." The woman stepped forward and extended her hand. "It's so good to finally meet you. Miranda Card."

Karas took her hand. "Miranda Card. What's this about a blue book?"

"And these"—Miranda looked at Johnis and Silvie—"are the two chosen ones: Johnis and Silvie."

"You know about us?" Johnis glanced at Silvie. "What do you know?"

"Only what Darsal told me," Miranda said. "Before she died."

"Darsal is dead?" Silvie asked. She wasn't sure what to make of the woman before them.

"Yes. I'm sorry, you have to forgive me. I never actually believed this day would come. It's all very strange to me." She smiled coyly, an expression mixed with some doubt and some intrigue. Her eyes rested on Johnis, and Silvie thought there might be some seduction behind her brown eyes as well.

They stared at her, stalled by the enormity of what the stranger named Miranda was suggesting.

"What are you trying to tell us?" Johnis asked. "That Darsal is dead, and you have her book?"

"I'm sorry, yes; I know it must come as a shock. But you have to understand that this is all a bit shocking to me as well."

"Why don't we sit?" Karas led them to a couch and two chairs that overlooked the city. "Now, perhaps you could start at the beginning. Tell us how you know Darsal and how you knew to look for us."

"Of course. Forgive me . . ." She wasn't able to wipe the faintest of grins from her face.

"No need to apologize," Silvie snapped. "Just tell us."

"I'm an American who works as the curator for a large private museum in Turkey, where Darsal first found me."

"Why was she looking for you?"

"She wasn't. She came to the library seven years ago, asking about for—"

"Seven years ago?" Silvie looked at Karas. "She's been here that long?"

"Longer," Miranda said. "She told me she'd come into this reality three years earlier on a quest to find the lost books. At first I thought she was a nutcase, you understand."

The woman withdrew a box of the white smoking sticks that

Karas called "cigarettes," lit one with a gold fire-starter, and blew smoke into the night air.

Still that slight grin.

"You find this humorous?" Silvie asked.

"I just flew five thousand miles to meet with you," Miranda said. "I think that earns me the right to express my nerves any way I wish, don't you?"

Silvie decided she didn't like this woman.

"Go on," Johnis said.

Miranda sucked on the cigarette and blew more smoke. "Let me start over. Your friend Darsal came to me in a state of desperation, suffering what I assumed were delusions of the grandest kind. End-of-the-world nonsense. The Dark One this, the lost books that. Alucard."

Johnis was on his feet. "He's here?"

"No. Not that I've seen. Sit."

He sat.

"She had a blue book that she claimed had transported her from another reality. She had to find six others and return them to the Roush. She was looking for three warriors: Karas, Johnis, and Silvie. I dismissed it all until she came to my house in the middle of the night, bleeding badly from a wound in her neck. 'A bite,' she claimed. She wouldn't let me call for medical help, so I did my best. She died the next morning on my kitchen table."

"You let her die?"

"She refused a trip to the hospital. I had no choice, trust me. Darsal wasn't the kind of woman you pushed around."

"You . . . she just died on your table and you didn't report it to the authorities?"

"I did. They cremated her body after an autopsy that confirmed she'd been bitten by an animal and perished from blood loss."

"But she gave you her blue book and told you about us," Karas said. "So why didn't you contact me sooner?"

"I can't say I truly believed her until I saw Johnis and Silvie on the Net, speaking of the books in the exact same way Darsal did. Needless to say, I was shocked. I left immediately."

"Where is it?" Karas demanded.

Miranda stared at the younger woman, dropped her smoke stick on the marble, and ground it out with a high-heeled black shoe.

"Darsal made me promise two things before she died. That I would never so much as show the book she left to any person without first confirming they had the others. And that I was to give the book to Johnis only and offer to help."

The curator from Turkey slid one leg over the other and waited for them to react.

Karas crossed her legs in similar fashion. "Then give Johnis the blue book. It's the only help we need."

Miranda smiled at her for a few long beats, then stood and crossed behind the couch. "Listen to you, refusing help from a friend who owes a debt. If Darsal was right, you already have your share of enemies, lurking out there in the night."

She ran her hand along the back cushion. A finger over Johnis's shoulder. "So beautiful and innocent, yet so naive."

"Bold for a woman standing in my house," Karas said.

"Take your hand off of him!" Silvie shouted.

Miranda continued, drawing her hand along his shoulder as she walked past. "She was very specific," she said. "According to Darsal, the presence of four books in this reality makes the final three visible. I'm assuming that to now be the case. But she also said that if the four books are brought, they can open a gateway back into the other reality. Now, you understand my reluctance to just hand over that kind of power to anyone."

"We are Johnis, Silvie, and Karas!" Johnis said. "What else do you need?"

"The books," Miranda said. "Show me the other three books, and convince me you have a plan to recover the final three, and I'll give you the fourth. I assure you it's only a matter of precaution."

Miranda might have stumbled onto Darsal's book, but she was still a seductive tramp, and the faster they satisfied her curiosity and got rid of her, the better, Silvie thought.

"Fine. Show her the books, Karas."

Johnis nodded.

Karas eyed the woman cautiously, then retreated into her mansion, to the vault that she'd shown them earlier.

Miranda leaned up against the railing and smoked another

cigarette. She stared at the mansion, ignoring them as if they didn't exist.

"I don't trust her," Silvie whispered.

"Think about it; she's playing her cards right."

"What do you mean, 'right'? She's a tramp!"

"Please, Silvie, she's sitting on what she now knows is a very powerful book. She's testing us, playing the tramp, throwing us off center."

"To what end? That's ridiculous."

"People reveal their true character when they're off center. You have to at least admire her tactics."

"Bah! I don't buy it."

Karas glided toward them, holding the wooden box. "Where is your book?" she asked.

"Show me," Miranda said, stepping up to the table.

"Are we complete imbeciles?" Johnis said. "Prove that you have the blue book."

Miranda eyed him. Smiled. She reached into her purse, pulled out an object bound in aging white cloth, and set it on the table.

Johnis unwrapped the blue Book of History and set it down gingerly. It could be a fake, but if so, it was a perfect replica. Silvie didn't think there was a way to prove the authenticity of the book without actually using it.

"Looks real."

"Of course it's real," Miranda said. "Now yours."

Johnis nodded.

Karas pulled the black, the brown, and the green Books of History out and laid them next to each other on the glass table. They stared at them in silence.

"So . . ." Miranda finally said. "Tell me how you're planning to find the other three."

"You think it's wise to discuss that in front of her?" Silvie demanded.

"Discuss what?" Johnis said. "We don't even have a plan. Admittedly, she's come off like a rude tramp." He turned to her and shrugged. "Sorry, but it's true." Back to Silvie, "But that doesn't make her wrong."

What could she say to that?

"I don't like her attitude," Karas said.

"She brought us the blue book," Johnis said. "You don't have to like her attitude. Or her hairstyle or the way she's dressed, for that matter. She makes a point. What is our next move?"

Karas sighed. "The subject of my dreams for ten years. I only know details of the mission from what Darsal shared on Other Earth, and she wasn't the most forthcoming, being so consumed with Billos. But I've also pieced together a few details from the people in Paradise, Colorado, that might help us."

"Such as?"

She sat. "I told you about the simulation called Paradise earlier, the one we entered by touching the cover of the book with blood."

"Yes."

"I dug up everything I could get my hands on about Paradise, Colorado, and I found more. It seems to be some kind of epicenter for the books, not only in the simulation, but also in reality."

"Darsal mentioned Paradise," Miranda said. "Only to say that it was the first place she searched before going to Turkey."

"And?"

"Nothing. 'A small town that refuses to grow up,' she said."

"Maybe there's a reason it refuses to grow up. Follow me here. We know that Thomas Hunter spared this world from impending disaster in 2010, roughly twenty-three years ago, right?"

"Right," Johnis said, though he couldn't possibly know this level of detail. "As you say." Better.

"What very few know is that an incident occurred in Paradise eleven years later—the year 2021. An experiment in a monastery dubbed 'Project Showdown,' in which thirty-six children were raised in a kind of utopian environment, spared from evil. But the whole thing went terribly wrong."

"How does this fit into the seven missing books?" Johnis asked.

"It's rumored that the children in the monastery had access to magical books"—she looked at Miranda—"from Turkey."

"The Books of History?"

"I think Thomas Hunter brought some Books of History into this reality," Karas said. "And among them were the books we seek."

"In Paradise?"

"It's a starting point," Karas said. "Think about it, the history of the world rests in the hands of the choices we make. My own history changed when I chose to bathe in the lake water. It's the will of men that Teeleh seeks. Paradise is made or corrupted depending on the choices of children and the evil character they shudder to think about. A priest gone bad: Marsuvees Black."

"So the quest for the books was always about saving this place, not the forests?" Silvie asked.

"Perhaps. And maybe Paradise is the epicenter. Paradise, perfection. In our history there is a number that represents perfection."

"Seven," Miranda said.

Karas nodded. "The seven lost books." She shrugged. "It's a thought anyway."

Silvie was still stuck on the suggestion that their entire mission was about saving this reality rather than saving the forests from the Horde.

"If the mission has always been about this reality," Johnis said, tracking with her, "then who is the Dark One? This 'Black' character?"

"That's the question, isn't it?"

Crickets chirped in the darkness.

"So," Miranda said, and they all looked at her. "You'll take up your search in this town of yours—Paradise, Colorado." The moon was high now, and the woman's face was pale by its light. As were her arms and hands, Silvie saw. She was a curator, who rarely saw the light of day.

Karas shook her head. "Actually, no. Not the town. I've scoured it high and low, and the monastery is gone. I'm more interested in the history of the books that destroyed Paradise." Her eyes settled on Miranda. "And those books came from Turkey."

"Oh?"

"But that's enough. We've said enough for you to know, without a shadow of a doubt, that we are who we say we are and are committed to finding the books. You can leave this book with us."

"Yes, of course. But first, Darsal insisted that I tell the chosen one something. That would be Johnis."

"We're all chosen," Silvie snapped.

"Johnis. She was quite specific. Come."

Johnis stood still, clearly unsure about the way she'd ordered him.

"Don't be afraid. Come here."

He walked up to her tentatively.

Silvie saw her move a split second before the weapon was in Miranda's hand. She whipped a gun hidden in her loose slacks like a striking snake and leveled it at his head.

"Can the chosen one dodge bullets?" Miranda asked sweetly. "I don't think so. No one moves, or he dies."

A dull thumping beat at the air then swelled to a pounding that buffeted the night.

Miranda smiled. "We're going to find out just how much power these books have. If Darsal was right, the world as we know it is about to change."

A helicopter rose over the edge of the pool—how it had remained undetected or from where it had come, Silvie didn't know, but she could see that Karas was dumbfounded.

Two warriors in black hung from either door, their weapons trained on Silvie and Karas. The flying beetle hovered ten feet from Miranda, who smiled gently.

"Do something, Silvie. Let me send at least one of you to join Darsal." And Silvie knew she would at the slightest excuse.

Miranda walked to the table, scooped up all of the books except the one she'd brought, and stepped back, maintaining her sights on Johnis.

"You can keep that blue book; it's worthless. Into the bird, baby." She waved the gun at the helicopter. "Now!"

Silvie knew she had to do something. But it was all happening too quickly, and she half-expected Karas to stop the tramp! Silvie stood rooted to the ground, her mind blank. Johnis stared, pleading for her to save him.

"Teeleh's lair," he said.

Miranda lowered her gun a few inches and pulled the trigger. A projectile tugged at Johnis's jeans, but he did not move, did not even flinch. Blood seeped from the superficial wound.

"Go on, Silvie," Miranda sneered. "Go for one of those knives in your pocket. Move, Johnis, or I go higher."

"Teeleh's lair, Silvie," he said. "Tell Karas every—"

"Silence!"

Johnis turned and walked to the helicopter.

Silvie took a step forward, her heart hammering, ready to throw herself at the woman backing to the bird.

"No, Silvie," Karas said. "Not now."

"No, Silvie," Miranda cried over the slicing blades. "Not now, not ever." She slid into the cabin, and the aircraft rose. It chopped higher into the night sky and faded into the darkness, leaving them speechless.

"We've lost the books," Karas said.

Silvie whirled on the young girl who'd grown up overnight. "The books? You have all the power in the world, and you let this tramp into your house to take Johnis?"

"Easy . . ."

"How dare you?" she screamed, trembling from head to foot. "How dare you let them take him? He's all I have!"

"Your emotions, Silvie." Karas walked up to her. "Please, I'm sorry . . ."

Silvie felt her hand move before she could stop herself. Felt the sting of her palm as it struck the older girl's cheek.

For a moment they stared at each other, Silvie breathing steadily through her rage, Karas standing white with a red cheek.

Karas stepped forward, opening her arms.

I've lost him, Silvie thought. *I've lost Johnis . . .*

Then she dropped her head onto Karas's shoulder and began to weep.

sixteen

Whoever Miranda Card was, she seemed to have adequate resources at her disposal, Johnis thought. He doubted any average human in the Histories had access to helicopters and jets like the one he'd been hustled into.

The two assistants that worked for the woman had strapped a muzzle over his mouth, fixed a blindfold on his head, clamped shackles on his hands and feet, and shoved him into the dark compartment in which he now lay. The whole abduction, from the time they'd left the ground at Karas's home to the time they'd switched over to the jet and taken to the air once again, had been a half hour at most. No sign of Miranda Card.

Johnis lay on his side, telling himself to remain calm. His nerves were sending fear through his system—more than he was accustomed to. He kept telling himself it was the air here, as Karas had said. He'd faced the Shataiki and felt less fear.

Then again, maybe he had reason to feel more fear now than when he'd faced Teeleh. He was in the belly of a flying beast far above the ground, being flown to the far reaches of an earth stuck in the Histories, far from anything remotely familiar to him.

And if that wasn't enough cause for alarm, there was the fact that they'd managed to hand all four books over to an enemy about whom they knew next to nothing other than her clear intent to use the books for harm. It had to be the doing of Alucard. He'd killed Darsal and then corrupted the woman who'd taken her book.

A door opened. Slammed shut. Fingers pulled the blindfold up to his forehead.

Miranda Card stood above him, expressionless except for a wicked flash in her eyes. She'd changed into a charcoal dress with thin straps over each shoulder, black lacy underclothing peeking below the hem at her knees. Instead of high heels, she wore black leather boots with dark grey socks. Black rubber straps circled her neck and wrists. A tattoo of a serpent crawled along her right shoulder.

She tugged the muzzle free and shoved a bowl of water toward him with her foot. "Drink. I don't need you dead yet."

Johnis had no appetite for water, not with this creature lording over him. She was worse than the Shataiki—at least they were inhuman beasts given to the destruction of good. But this one . . .

A human who'd turned. Like Tanis. Like the Horde. It was no wonder that the people of the Histories would come to a nasty end, as was spoken of in hushed tones around campfires—more than mere legends.

"I'm sorry your travels between the worlds had to come to such an abrupt end so soon, but I've been patient enough."

"You're bluffing; you only have three of the books," he said.

"I assure you, I have the blue book, complete with the smudge of Darsal's blood on the first page. I not only have it; I've used it to enter the simulation—Paradise—many times. I assume you know about the simulation. The skin of this world."

"I've been there once. The man in the desert."

"Oh, that—Red, one of Black's creations gone rogue. As was White. Never mind them. I have all four books now, which is the key to the final three."

"You're underestimating Karas," Johnis said. "She's probably already on a jet, chasing you down."

"Is that so? To where?"

"Turkey."

Miranda grinned, then flattened her mouth. "Turkey is where the books were collected before they went to the monastery. They disappeared again, but not to Turkey; I've exhausted my search there."

"Then where?"

Miranda walked to the door, opened it, and stepped outside. "Romania," she said, and shut him into pitch darkness once again.

THE FLIGHT LASTED FOR MANY HOURS, AND AT ONE POINT Johnis was sure they would perish. The flying contraption bounced around like a tube strapped to a stallion's rear quarters. He cried out in alarm a dozen times, begging for Elyon to take him quickly, but if anyone was listening, he neither responded nor settled the bucking ship.

It occurred to him after an hour of being thrown about that they must be under attack. Karas had found them and was giving chase! It was the only possible explanation. Surely she realized that if the jet crashed to the ground, he would go with it! But when they finally hauled him from the craft in the dead of night, no one showed any concern of having narrowly escaped disaster.

They bound him in the back of a square, black car and sped through darkness, led by another car that carried Miranda Card. "Bucharest," one of them said, when Johnis asked where they were. And then, with a chuckle, "Welcome to hell."

Johnis still had some advantages they might not know about. His speed, his strength. His superior intelligence, although according to Karas, his mind would need time to make the adjustment.

Neither his speed nor his strength offered any advantage as long as they kept him in shackles. They seemed to have taken all the necessary precautions.

The large car left the city lights behind and climbed laboriously up a winding road that quickly turned rough. Dirt rather than concrete. A light fog settled over the mountain, but the headlamps pierced it with thick chords of light. The longer they traveled, the less talking took place between the driver and his guard. Soon the only sounds were the engine's whine and crunching gravel under the wheels.

When they finally stopped and turned off the engine, the air felt heavy, or was it the silence? The fog had thinned, and he could see the colossal citadel towering over them, barely visible against the dark sky. No lights. And no windows to allow light out.

Miranda walked in ahead of him. They shoved him forward, forcing him to take small, quick steps to avoid tripping on the shackles.

He stumbled through huge wooden doors that thudded shut behind him. Miranda's hard-soled shoes echoed down the torch-lit stone hall.

"There is no escape, chosen one. Follow me." Her voice dripped with spite.

Johnis followed, his heart pounding with each clank of his chains. Down the hall, into a stairwell that curved as it fell into the ground. He stopped at the entrance to several tunnels and lifted his arm to his nose. The odor was unmistakable: Shataiki.

He'd been in Teeleh's lair. Then Alucard's lair. And now another lair, here in the Histories: Romania.

"Move!"

He obeyed. Mucus covered the walls. No worms, but they were near; all of this sludge had come from somewhere. He shivered and forced his legs to move on, toward his objective.

It was true, no matter how much fear coursed through his

veins, he was as much drawn by purpose as pushed by his enemy's demands now. He'd come to the Histories to destroy evil, not flee from it!

The thought gave him some courage, but not much.

Miranda disappeared through a gate ahead on his right. He slowed, listening. Very soft popping sounds ran up and down the tunnel. But by peering into the light cast by the wall sconces, he could see only more darkness beyond.

The iron gate rested open, and he stepped cautiously through. A couch, a desk, bookshelves mostly empty. But unlike Teeleh's or Alucard's lair, this study had a large opening in the back. Another tunnel glowed with flickering flame. Water dripped far away.

He hesitated only a moment, then headed in. The floor sloped down, deeper into the ground. For a few steady breaths, he seriously considered turning and running, but he knew that there was no escape.

So he pushed his legs on. Further. Deeper.

The tunnel opened into a large, two-story library lit by wall torches and a half-dozen candelabras rising from dark wooden tables at the center. Wrought-iron railings ran the perimeter of the second floor and opened to the large atrium in which Johnis had entered.

Thousands of books lined the shelves on either side, but the wall directly ahead was draped with red velvet swags. A single table was framed by the heavy drapes. Twin candlesticks, each forming a winged serpent, sat on the table: Teeleh's symbol.

Miranda stood before the table, her back toward him. She turned and walked to one side, giving him full view of the table. The four books lay one on top of the other—black, brown, blue, green.

"Welcome to my world," Miranda said.

Johnis looked at the woman standing like a warrior in a dress, boots, and long, stringy hair. She looked as if she might be sick.

"Your world or his world?" Johnis asked.

"Is there a difference?"

"You don't know what you've gotten yourself into."

"And I would say it's you who have no idea what you've stumbled into. If Darsal was right, you were nothing but a poet a few weeks ago, rejected by this Forest Guard of yours. Your little quest is only four weeks old, isn't that right?"

So much had happened that it felt much longer. "Yes, that's right."

"Here in the so-called Histories, the quest for the books' power is over two thousand years old." Miranda's lips twisted in a whimsical smile. "You're but the latest little blip in a very long and gruesome ordeal that's lasted centuries. Darsal stumbled into something much larger than she could possibly know. As have you. The truth is, you know nothing, little Johnis." Then much louder, even furious, "*Nothing!*"

"I know where *he* comes from!" Johnis gestured toward the candlesticks. "Who he is. What he's capable of."

Miranda chuckled and walked slowly past the table, brushing

the four books with her fingertips. "Really? Then tell me even one thing you know so well. Tell me who he is?"

"The Dark One: Alucard."

"The nasty beast, Alucard. And what do you really know about Alucard?"

"That Teeleh sent him here to deceive the likes of you, which he's done surprisingly well in such a short time."

Miranda walked back, her hands now behind her back like a lecturer. Grinning at the fool. "You see, already you're misinformed. Alucard has been here for two thousand years, sowing seeds of misery and darkness in more ways than you've imagined."

She let the statement settle.

"And although he's a nasty beast around whom a whole mythology has emerged, spawning hundreds of stories about vampires and creatures of the night and all such things, he's not this 'Dark One' Darsal went on and on about. Not in this world, anyway. For that matter, neither is Marsuvees Black. Nor Red nor White . . . nor any of the other minions."

"Who then?"

"Unfortunately, you'll never know." Miranda's eyes settled on the table, and for the first time Johnis saw a silver knife resting beside the four books. "I do believe he intends to kill you the same way he killed Darsal seven years ago."

She picked up the knife and pulled the blade out of its silver sheath. "Not with a knife; he prefers another, more intimate method that's well-known in this world."

An image of Darsal bleeding to death from a neck bite blossomed in Johnis's mind. He'd never heard of the Shataiki killing that way. Then again, until a few weeks ago, the Shataiki were hardly more than legend in a world far away.

"You cannot thwart the will of Elyon," he said with as much confidence as he could muster.

"Elyon? You haven't heard? God is dead in this world. They killed him two thousand years ago. Alucard was there."

Johnis had no clue what Miranda referred to, but it hardly mattered any longer. His task was a simple one, and he had no intention of allowing her to complicate things.

"Why did you bring me here?"

"Because I asked her to," a voice rasped from above.

Johnis jerked his head up and stared at the rafters. The diseased, batlike creature hung from the center beam, staring down with yellow eyes.

Alucard.

He hid himself among thick worms, like a mother nesting her eggs. Slowly he unfolded himself, then dropped from the ceiling and landed on the library floor next to Miranda. Eyes on Johnis.

Alucard's mangy skin was whiter than he remembered, covered with mucus now, and his eyes had turned yellow. Otherwise two thousand years hadn't changed the beast.

"Hello, Johnisssss . . ."

seventeen

"Teeleh's Lair."

Silvie paced, biting at her fingernail. "What was he thinking? We all went into Alucard's lair, but Johnis was the only one who went into Teeleh's beneath the lake. It was where he found the brown book."

"There has to be more than you've told me," Karas said. "Why else would he tell you to tell me? You have to *think*!"

"I'm trying to!" Silvie shouted. "But something about this air, this cursed world . . . I can't think straight! I thought we were supposed to be more intelligent, not less!"

"Calm down, I'm not the enemy here. And the intelligence will come; have patience. It may take a few days, a couple weeks—"

"We don't have a couple weeks!"

"Then sit down and think with me! Start at the beginning."

"Again?"

"Again!"

The night had crawled by in relentless fits of tears and threats to end it all here and now. They had to give chase, never mind that they didn't know where to—just go. They had to inform the authorities, never mind that the police would likely send them both off to the fruit farm. They had to offer money, information, cars, whatever was necessary to purchase Johnis's life back, never mind that they didn't know who to offer it to.

The eastern sky had grayed with dawn, and now even Karas was showing signs of panic, which didn't help matters. Silvie dropped onto the couch that faced Los Angeles, which was spread out like an endless gray canyon before them. Her head spun with the events of the past week. They'd gone from celebrated heroes in the forest to insignificant fruits in the Histories in a matter of days.

"It's hopeless," she said. "Look at that."

"I do," Karas said. "Nearly every day."

"Thousands and thousands of buildings. Millions of people. Cars and airplanes and endless miles of stone or concrete or asphalt or whatever you call it. Fortunes being made and lost, rock stars getting their feet kissed, ordinary people eating and dressing and dreaming. And here we sit, like two ants on the hill, thinking we must or can do something to change any of it. You don't ever feel helpless?"

"Completely," Karas said. "Try doing it for ten years . . ."

"Right." She looked at Karas. "None of them even know that there are seven Books of History that can reshape reality as they know it."

"No. But some of them wouldn't be surprised."

"Where we come from, one day's events could change everything. Are there ever earth-shattering incidents here? Wars that change everything? Outcomes that every man, woman, and child leans forward to hear?"

"Not really, no. But everyone knows it will happen one day."

"Could they imagine that it *is* happening? Right now. Today!"

"Some," she sighed. "Please, Silvie. I know you're not thinking straight. You've been uprooted; we've lost the books; Johnis is gone . . ."

"He kissed me, Karas." She felt the tears seep into her eyes and made no attempt to blink them away. "We have fallen in love. I know it's foolish for members of the Forest Guard, and I know we are only just of marrying age, but I would marry him. Nothing else matters to me anymore."

"The books . . ."

"What about you, Karas? You're twenty-one. Surely you've fallen in love."

"More than once."

"I mean, look at you! You're stunning. What's wrong with the men in the Histories? They should be lined up outside your door!"

"Well, that's not how we do things here, but they are." She

looked far off. "But I've been a little too preoccupied to entertain more than a passing interest."

Spoken like the principled little girl who'd broken ranks with the Horde at great risk to herself—almost a reprimand.

"Perhaps if I had someone like Johnis . . ."

"Don't even think about it!"

"Don't be ridiculous," Karas said, blushing. "I know when I'm beat. Unfortunately, men from our world are in short supply here."

Silvie felt bad for the girl.

"Well, I have a feeling that everything's going to change in the very near future." Silvie took a deep breath and blew it out slowly. "Okay, let's start at the beginning. What did Johnis mean, 'Teeleh's lair'? He wanted to say something that I would understand without Miranda's knowledge."

"She's after the same thing we are now: the final three books."

"Which became accessible when Johnis crossed over with the fourth book."

"Right, we've been over this." Karas stood and walked up to the railing. "Teeleh's lair . . . it's the key to the location, Silvie. Something he told you that no one else could know."

"I told you. He described it to me in the desert on the way to the Horde City. And from what I can remember, it's exactly the same as Alucard's lair except . . ."

Silvie's heart stopped. She jumped to her feet.

"What?" Karas asked.

"The poem! He said there was a poem on the wall. I don't

remember anything in Alucard's lair. That's what was unique about Teeleh's lair. He must have been trying to direct me to the poem without tipping off Miranda!"

Karas hurried over, her eyes wide. "What poem?"

"Something about a sinner, a saint, and a showdown." She blinked. "'Welcome to Paradise.'"

"It said that? 'Welcome to Paradise'?"

"Yes."

"Yes, okay, yes. So what does—"

And then Karas got it.

"Paradise. The epicenter of this showdown between saint and sinner, good and evil. You're saying that there is a lair in Paradise."

"'Welcome to Paradise,'" Silvie repeated.

"The monastery was destroyed. Flattened. I've been there. Nothing but a cabin."

"But were you looking for Teeleh's lair? Johnis must have . . ." Her voice trailed off.

Karas stared at her in silence, piecing together what she'd just learned with what she already knew.

She suddenly rushed toward the house. "Get the jet up!" she cried to one of her servants inside.

Silvie hurried behind. "To where?"

"Paradise, Colorado."

eighteen

Alucard's tongue licked at the mucus on his fingers. He stared at Johnis like a mad doctor who'd trapped a monkey on which to run his forbidden experiments.

"The beast from hell," Johnis said. Although he meant it as an accusation, his voice came out strained.

"I have waited for this day." Alucard walked to the table, his talons clicking on the stone floor. He reached out and touched the prize Miranda had delivered.

"Four is a far cry from seven," Johnis said.

"That's where you're wrong, my friend. Finding the last three will be a simple matter now. They may be the prize locked away for centuries, but I now have the key." He faced Johnis, his lips twisted. "Surely you know where the other three are."

Johnis had his ideas, to which he'd tried to alert Silvie. But he knew more than Alucard could possibly know.

"There are only a few lairs in this reality. For all we know, the last three books are hidden here, in this very library." His eyes ran over the bookcases. Johnis wasn't positive that the books were in a lair, but they seemed to favor lairs on Other Earth.

After two thousand years, Alucard wasn't in a rush to tear the place apart, Johnis realized. If the last three books were in one of the lairs, he wasn't in any danger of someone else finding them before he did. Except for Silvie and Karas.

A chuckle echoed softly around the room. Alucard walked around him, moving easily, inspecting. "You're wondering why I didn't just kill all three of you? Are you really so foolish?"

The stench of the beast's flesh so close was enough to make Johnis temper his breathing.

"Tell him, Miranda."

"We can kill them at any time. Why would we eliminate something that could still be useful?" She spoke as if she were a disinterested peer to the Shataiki, not his servant.

How so? Johnis wanted to ask. But he already knew. They'd taken him in the event they needed leverage. "What makes you think Silvie and Karas won't find the books before you do?"

"Let them. It is now only a matter of time. Hours, days, it makes no difference to me." Alucard breathed heavily and continued in a soft voice that trembled with each word. "My time has come."

The worms overhead moved through their own muck, agitated.

"We have waited so long. Unlike you humans, Shataiki are born of the hive lord, the equivalent of your queen bee, only male. All we need now are the females."

Johnis shuddered. These worms were Alucard's offspring, trapped larvae, waiting for a female to somehow make them Shataiki. Or was Alucard the female? Either way, with the four books, Alucard could return to the Black Forest and bring back what he needed to turn these larvae into Shataiki. And what would happen to this world if thousands of Shataiki were set free?

"You . . . you can't do that."

"And now that you know how your little quest is going to end, I can kill you." Alucard's long, sharp talon reached around Johnis's neck from behind and drew a thin line over his exposed skin. One jerk and his head would be parted from his body. Was the beast's need to see the chosen one dead greater than his need for any leverage Johnis might give him?

Johnis didn't want to find out.

The talon bit into his skin. "Are you ready to die, chosen one?"

"You can't." He looked at Miranda's dark stare. "You don't have four of the books."

The talon at his neck hesitated.

"Don't be a fool," Miranda said.

"Am I the fool? Do you think we are that stupid?"

A tick bothered Miranda's cheek.

"You have four books on the table," Johnis said. "Three of them are genuine. One of them is a fake."

THE JET STREAKED FOR THE SKY, AND SILVIE GRIPPED THE armrests, her knuckles white. But once again, the flying tube of steel hung in the air as comfortably as any bird she'd seen.

She slowly released her grip. "What if we're wrong?"

"We're not," Karas said. "The books are in Teeleh's lair, wherever that is. I'm willing to stake my life on it."

"It's his life you're staking. What's all this numbers business?"

"Six of the books went missing. The number of evil, perfection divided. Three are now missing: the number that Teeleh aspires to become—perfection. Follow?"

"Not really."

"Then never mind for now. The point is, the three missing books are almost certainly hidden in the heart of darkness. Teeleh's lair."

"But what makes you think there aren't other 'hearts of darkness' here in the Histories? Why tie it directly to Teeleh?"

"Because you said it yourself, 'Welcome to Paradise.' Because the books came from our world when Thomas Hunter crossed over. They would naturally find a place consistent with that world—Teeleh's lair."

"Three books in our world; three here," Silvie said, as if it now all made perfect sense to her. "Six missing books. Evil. Perfection defiled. And if we're wrong about the lair being in Paradise?"

Karas frowned. "Then we hope Johnis has something up his sleeve besides a little extra strength."

"HE'S LYING," MIRANDA SNAPPED.

Johnis allowed himself a moment of satisfaction. "Now who's the fool?"

Alucard whipped around him and leaped to the table, where he landed on his hind legs with enough force to send a vibration through the floor. He fanned the books across the table with a flip of his wrist. "Show me!"

Miranda was already hovering over the books, the silver knife in her hand. She shoved the blue book to the side and pulled the brown book closer—sliced her finger.

Holding her eyes on Johnis, she planted her finger on the brown book's cover.

She vanished in a wink of light into this simulation they talked about, modeled after Paradise. Everyone wants a piece of Paradise.

The brown book lay still, smudged with Miranda's blood. Alucard stood by the table, breathing steadily. The worms squirmed slowly above. Johnis stood in his shackles.

A silent flash of light appeared over the book, and Miranda stood next to the table again, wearing a smirk. "Works for me."

She pushed the brown book aside and pressed her finger against the green one.

Again, a wink of light swallowed her.

Alucard grunted.

The woman reappeared. Still smiling.

"The black one," the Shataiki growled.

Miranda brushed the green book aside and pulled the black one closer. She shoved her finger against the cover.

Nothing happened.

"Cut yourself!" Alucard said.

Her finger was no longer bleeding. She snatched up the silver knife they evidently kept for this very purpose and cut her skin again. Red blood seeped from the fresh wound.

She smashed it against the cover.

But Miranda did not vanish. What Karas had told him was true: she'd made a duplicate book and hidden the original. Today her effort paid off.

Alucard snarled and rushed the ten feet to Johnis. His claw squeezed around Johnis's neck. Unable to breathe, much less scream, Johnis could only clench his eyes against the pain.

"Where is the fourth book?"

The beast's breath was hot and wet.

"Give me the book!"

"Killing him won't help us!" Miranda said. "Let him go."

Alucard held him for another five seconds, then relaxed his grip. He backhanded Johnis with enough force to throw him backward several feet.

He landed on his side, struggling for breath.

"Where is it?" Alucard repeated.

He would die before he told them. Now it was only about stalling to give Silvie more time. Johnis coughed. Blood wet the stone by his hand. Alucard had damaged his throat. He lay on the dungeon floor, broken.

Hopelessness came, like an avalanche in the night, thundering down on him from overhead. He was going to fail. This beast was far too powerful to stop!

There was only one play left for him.

"He doesn't know," Alucard said. "Kill him."

"No," Johnis gasped. "I do know!"

Miranda stooped beside him and traced his cheek with her knife. "Of course you know. Karas would tell the chosen one. You know. And we know where Silvie is headed. We don't need her; Karas will suffice. One word and Silvie will die."

"Don't . . . You can't harm her!"

"This is a waste of time," Alucard snarled. "Lock this useless slab of meat up. Cut off his leg and show it to her. If she still doesn't cooperate, kill her and work on the little runt."

"No, I can take you to the book."

"Or lead me astray." Miranda's knife lingered just beneath his jaw. "To buy your little lover more time?"

It occurred to Johnis that Miranda always spoke as if it was she, not Alucard, who should be dealt with here. As if she, not the beast, held the true power in the room. At least in her mind.

"Just tell me," she said.

"I can't. But I can take you. If you don't get the book, kill me. But leave Silvie. You have me! What can you gain by taking her now?"

Plenty.

Miranda smiled, drawing the knife across his cheek. Then she nicked him. "Don't flirt with the illusion that you've bought yourself more than a few more hours of life. It's all going to end soon."

She turned her back on him and spoke to Alucard. "I have reason to believe that the other three books may be in the buried monastery."

He grunted softly. "We'll see. Bring me her book."

nineteen

Paradise sat in the valley directly below the helicopter. A sleepy-looking village with only one paved street that she could see.

"Hardly the kind of place you'd expect to be the epicenter of the struggle between good and evil," Silvie said.

"I think that's the point."

Since there was no place to land a jet in Paradise, they'd flown into a town named Grand Junction, then switched to the helicopter Karas had arranged.

"There's something you should know, Silvie," Karas said, staring at the town below them. "I've been debating whether to tell you because I'm afraid that they will stop at nothing to get the information from one of us if they take us. I already made a mistake in telling Johnis."

"What are you talking about?"

Karas looked at her. "My book, the one Miranda took, was a copy. Mine is hidden in Paradise. I'm sorry for not telling you sooner. But Miranda only has three books, not four."

Silvie didn't know what to think about the prospect of her trusting Johnis, but at the moment she didn't feel the need to dwell on it. There were more important matters at hand.

"Fine. It's safe, right? Probably the safest place for it right now."

"Unless Johnis—"

"He wouldn't. And Miranda may have pieced together what we have about the other three. We should test our theory first and return if we find them."

"Or we could hide my book again to protect Johnis."

"We have to see if there's a lair," Silvie snapped.

"Okay. To the canyons."

The helicopter floated over Paradise, then headed into the canyon lands to the south. A wide, white-faced gorge had been cut from the mountain. They flew down into it and pulled up near the box canyon at the end.

"Where?"

"There." Karas pointed to a cliff on her side of the helicopter where a landslide had taken down a hundred yards of the canyon wall. "They used explosives to implode a monastery built into the cliff face. A real shame. Someone went to a lot of trouble to keep this place hidden."

A small cabin had been built among the rubble, but this didn't strike Silvie as the kind of place they would find the books that had caused them so much trouble.

"Take 'er down," Karas signaled the pilot.

They landed a hundred feet from the cabin and ducked out from under the spinning blades. "Wait for us."

Karas led Silvie through an unlocked cabin door, into what looked to be a long, deserted room with two doors leading farther in. They quickly checked the two rooms: nothing obvious.

Karas switched on her battery-operated torch and ran it over the floor. "Okay, we're looking for an opening that leads below the cabin."

Silvie tried her own light. She might have been mesmerized by the contraption—fire sealed in this battery Karas referred to—but her mind was preoccupied with Johnis's absence. "How do we know the lair is here, not buried under all the rubble?"

"We don't."

"Surely Alucard would have searched this place."

"Not since all four books have been in this reality, he hasn't."

"How do you know? He could be down there right now, waiting for us."

"Turkey, maybe. Or Romania. I doubt he's here."

"Romania?"

"Never mind. Come on."

They searched the outer room first, covering every square inch on their hands and knees. The whole business was enough to soak

Silvie in sweat. All she could think about was Johnis caged in a dungeon . . . or worse.

"We're wasting time!" Silvie announced, standing. "What was that you said about Romania? This can't be the right place!"

"I'll take one room; you take the other."

The *other* was a bathroom, and it took Silvie only a few minutes to convince herself that there was nothing remotely resembling Teeleh's lair within a hundred miles of this place.

"Silvie!"

She dove for the door, slammed into its frame, and spun through, ignoring the pain that flashed up her arm.

"What is it?"

She saw what it was before Karas could answer. The wood-frame bed had been pulled to one side, and a trapdoor rose to reveal a dark tunnel beneath.

They'd actually found it?

"There's a ladder." Silvie dove for the hole and was halfway into the floor before Karas could stop her.

"Easy! I have the gun. I should lead."

Silvie hesitated as Karas dropped past her into the earth below. They were in a small tunnel that ran perpendicular to the earth's surface, not deep. It was an escape route freshly dug, not an ancient fortified tunnel like Alucard's lair.

"This isn't it," she breathed, hurrying behind Karas, who scurried forward in a crouch, her gun extended.

No response.

They rounded a bend, following the light from their battery-operated torches. The tunnel ended at another ladder heading up. Light seeped through a square trapdoor about fifty feet above their heads.

"That's it?" Silvie looked back. "We missed something! There has to be another tunnel!"

She spun and headed back, chasing the sound of her breathing now. Miranda was torturing Johnis in a land far away, while they wasted their time here beneath a cabin outside Paradise, Colorado.

"Silvie!"

She plowed on. The quicker they covered this search and left Paradise, the better. Nothing here looked like Teeleh.

"Silvie!"

She spun back. "What?"

"Do you hear that?"

Silvie heard her own wheezing. Her thumping heart. "No."

"There, listen!"

Silvie held her breath and listened. Then she heard it, a very faint, high-pitched squealing sound that sent a streak of terror down her spine.

She studied the dirt ceiling. The walls. It seemed to come at them from every direction from far away. Her eyes met Karas's, round like saucers. The squealing was louder now that they were perfectly still.

"What is that?" Silvie breathed.

"I . . . I don't know." She shoved her gun into her belt, leaned her ear close to the wall, and listened. "It's . . ." But she didn't know more.

Silvie drew her light slowly over the rough dirt walls. She walked farther down the tunnel. The sounds faded.

She walked back slowly. "It's louder here. Something's behind the walls. There has to be . . ."

Silvie suddenly saw the demarcation along the tunnel wall, rockier along a five-foot section between her and Karas. She stepped up and placed her ear between the rocks.

The squealing was now distinct, like the wailing of a million insects or lobsters, protesting their capture.

"You're right," Karas said.

"What is it?"

"I don't know." She headed back down the tunnel. "But we're going to find out."

It took them nearly an hour to dig through the tunnel wall using shovels from the helicopter. Silvie swung her spade, fighting to hold her frustration in check. It was clear that Johnis wasn't here because the earth had been undisturbed for a long time.

The books probably weren't here either. They couldn't be so fortunate as to find them so quickly after arriving in the Histories. Then again, Karas had been searching for over ten years. She and Johnis had just shown up near the end of the search. Either way, something was here. The more they dug, the louder the squealing sounded.

"We should just use dynamite and be done with this!" Karas mumbled.

"Dynamite?" Silvie pried up on a rock, attempting to pluck it from the earth, but it remained stuck. "What's dynamite?"

The rock suddenly rolled. Not toward her, but away. Into darkness beyond.

The squealing became a faint, but much clearer, high-pitched screaming. Silvie went rigid. The sound of the boulder rolling down a slope was unmistakable. It landed far below with a dull thump.

The squealing stopped.

Karas scrambled for one of the torches. Shone it through the hole. The beam revealed nothing but darkness. And an eerie silence.

"Teeleh's lair?"

For the first time since landing in the canyon, Silvie felt a strong surge of hope. They'd certainly found something, and it could be Teeleh's lair.

Which meant the Books of History could be here. And the Books of History were their only leverage now. Johnis's life depended on what they found in this hole.

She dropped to her seat and kicked at the rocks surrounding the small hole. The wall caved as if the whole thing had been held up by a small toothpick. A small avalanche tumbled away from them.

Dust coiled.

Silvie grabbed her torch and crawled through the opening.

"What is it?" Karas asked from behind.

"A staircase. I . . . I don't know."

She eased out onto stone steps spiraling into darkness. No walls on either side or ahead that she could see. Silence.

Karas stood up beside her and played her light around. "A cavern below the old monastery. This has to be it, Silvie. Nothing else would explain this."

"Let's go." Silvie stepped gingerly around fallen rock, pushing stones aside as she descended. Fifty steps. Farther. Now a stench from below. A smell that reminded her of putrid water or . . .

She stopped. "Shataiki!" Her whisper echoed softly. She flashed her light up and saw a stone wall ahead, wet with mucus. And lying across the mucus was a large worm, perhaps a full foot in diameter. Twenty yards long.

Karas put a hand on her shoulder and held tight.

These were the same worms from Alucard's lair. Johnis had wondered if they might be larvae for the larger Shataiki, and looking at this one now, Silvie guessed he was right.

She wanted to spin, run back up the stairs, and drop fire in this hole to kill all that lived below. But Johnis . . .

Silvie clenched her jaw and stepped down, farther in.

The steps ended at the base of the wall. They were in a massive cavern, but she could only see this one wall. A single blackened wooden door hung from rusted hinges, gaping an inch or two.

"This is it." Her voice came raspy. "Is it safe?"

A stupid question, one that Karas didn't bother answering. She stepped past Silvie, her gun extended again. Still silence. So then what had done all the squealing? Karas drew the door wide with the gun's barrel.

A smaller atrium waited inside. And from this atrium several tunnels headed farther in. But the tunnel on their right was the one they should take. It was the only one with worms on the walls, slipping through their own mucus.

They held their torches on the same entrance, transfixed by the sight of two worms so close. And then the squealing came, louder than Silvie thought could have been possible from the small mouth on one of the worms, now open in a scream.

She jumped back. But other than moving its head about, the worm did nothing. No sign of threat other than this cry of protest. The halls fell quiet once more.

"They've been trapped down here," Karas said, "for Elyon knows how long. Waiting to be set free."

"By who?"

"Alucard? Maybe he couldn't do it without all seven books."

"If you're right," Silvie said, "and if he thinks he has the other four, he might be on his way now."

"So . . . we should go in."

They exchanged a look of fear, then walked forward into the tunnel.

The walls were strewn so thick with worms that they hid most of the stone. They waded through four inches of sludge covering the floor, only partially protected by their boots.

Silvie switched her torch to one hand and covered her nose

with the other. If the lair was laid out like Alucard's, the heart of the nest would be behind a set of gates, ahead on the right.

Which is where they found it. Gate locked. Empty of worms.

Their torches illuminated a study of sorts, complete with desk, a couch, and some bookcases. No dust, but plenty of worm salve. It was almost identical to the study in Alucard's lair. Slightly different furniture and arrangement, but clearly cut from the same blueprint.

"Stand back." Karas aimed the barrel of her gun at the lock, turned her head, and pulled the trigger. *Boom!*

Worms squealed. The lock lay in two. She wrestled it from the latch and opened the gate. With a screech of rusted hinges, the study opened to them.

"Are they here?" Silvie demanded.

Karas fired a stick and set the flame against an old torch mounted on the wall. The flame grew and crackled, spewing black smoke.

Orange light licked the glistening walls. Someone had carved an inscription into the rock next to the gate: *Welcome to Paradise, Population 450.*

"This is definitely what Billy wrote," Karas said.

"You mean 'Billos'?"

"No. One of the children in the monastery. It's a long story. But this is where the showdown all began. Or ended. Or is it still in full swing?"

"In my book it's still going," Silvie said. "Until we find Johnis and the books."

"So where are they?"

She turned, studying each corner. Silvie walked to the desk and pulled open one of two drawers on each side.

There, just visible in the shadows, lay an old black book. The words on its cover jumped out. Silvie gasped. Reached for the book and pulled it out. Bound in red twine exactly like the other four.

"I was right!" Karas cried. "They're here!"

But the drawer was empty. "They?"

Karas fumbled with the other drawer, yanked it open, staring inside. She reached in with both hands and pulled out two books, laying them on the desk beside Silvie's black one.

Purple and gold, bound by red twine, bearing the same name: *The Story of History.*

They'd found the three missing books.

"You know what this means?" Karas looked at her. "With the book I have hidden, we now have four. We have to collect the fourth book! We have to get down to Paradise!"

Silvie agreed. One problem: "They still have Johnis."

As one, the worms in the hall behind them began to screech.

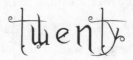

"Paradise? Why would she hide the book in Paradise, of all places? It's far too obvious."

"Not just anywhere in Paradise. You're saying you could just walk in, tear them apart, and take the books?"

"But Paradise. We've searched . . ."

"Maybe the fact that it's so obvious makes it the perfect place. Either way, you'll know soon enough."

"Tell me where."

"And minimize my value? I'll *show* you."

Miranda smiled gently, eyeing Johnis with interest. She was still dressed in the boots, the dark dress, the lace. Long, black, unkempt hair. A perfectly formed face that, apart from her betrayal, would be beautiful.

She sat beside him with her arms crossed and one leg draped over the other as the helicopter wound through the mountains, flying low. The flight from Romania had taken only a few hours aboard the orbital jet. The sun was beginning to dip in the west.

There was a strong possibility that Karas had already collected the book and, if so, Johnis was finished. But he also knew that both he and Silvie were finished anyway. His only hope was to stall Miranda long enough to give Karas time.

Time to find the last three books before Alucard could get his claws on them.

"You remind me of Darsal," Miranda said. "Both so intent, so obsessed with this mission."

"That's nice."

"She was bitter, you know. When I met her, she'd spent three years without success. She had no clue what had happened to the others. To you. But she was driven by something else entirely. Do you know what that was?"

"Billos," Johnis said.

"A man. She was in love with a man. She once told me that she blamed Elyon. It was his rules that forced Billos to give up his life."

"Billos died? She said that?"

"I suppose so. She obviously thought he was dead."

"And what did she expect to do about it?" Johnis demanded.

"That's the question, isn't it? What did she think having all seven books would do for her?"

Miranda's suggestion stunned him. This notion that Darsal might have intended to use the books for her own gain or for revenge . . . preposterous!

There had always been a strange connection between Darsal and Billos, dating back to his rescue of her when she was much younger. Clearly, whatever had happened when they'd both gone into the books had only strengthened the bond.

"Well?" Miranda pressed. "What could someone like Darsal or, for that matter, anyone do with the seven books?"

"Something in this world," Johnis said.

"Yes, this world. It's always been about this world. Even the Shataiki are about this world. They may have crossed some forbidden river, thanks to Tanis, as Alucard claims, but they've always had their sights on this world. And now they're about to repeat it, honey."

Some of what she said made sense; some it didn't. For Johnis, the matter was simple: he was here to get the books before the Dark One could. And so far he'd done that by following his heart.

"It's all about the Shataiki, and it's all about love." Miranda looked at him. "What about you, Johnis? What would you do for love?"

"Anything."

"I'm counting on it. You're just like Darsal that way." She rested her hand on his thigh. "I like that in a man."

"Take your stinking hands off me."

She leaned close. He could smell her perfume, a rich spice he didn't recognize. The scent of Shataiki lingered faintly about her.

"When I have the books, you'll change your tune, little boy. And make no mistake, I will have them."

"Don't you mean Alucard?"

"Alucard," she said slowly. "I'm sure you've figured out that it was he who killed Darsal. As he intends on killing you."

Her hand suddenly tightened like a vice above his knee. Her grip was strong, stronger than he thought possible.

She released him, lifted her hand, and slapped him with enough force to spin his head.

"Love, baby. It's all about love."

Two minutes later they settled in a field just behind a spire-tipped building Miranda called a "church," and Johnis's head was still spinning with her words. Her slap. He wasn't sure he shouldn't fear Miranda Card more than Alucard.

It was now all about timing. He would make his play, but not until they had the book. Then he would see just what this witch was made of. He had a few tricks up his sleeve himself.

"Where to?"

"To the home of Sally Drake," Johnis said.

"Let's go."

"You know where it is?"

"Like I said, I've been here in the simulation looking for clues. If you're wrong about this, I'm going to cut off your fingers. Start praying, boy."

"HURRY!"

Silvie stumbled over the stones that littered the top of the stairs. She glanced over her shoulder and saw that Karas, who carried the three Books of History, was still twenty steps behind. "Hurry!"

"This isn't a race!" Karas panted. "We have them, Silvie. You want me to lose them?"

Silvie played her light to the side. She had no idea how far it was to the bottom or if there *was* a bottom. "Just hurry; they have Johnis."

"Having the books won't help us find Johnis."

You're wrong, Karas. The books are exactly what we need to find Johnis. She spilled through the hole they'd punched in the tunnel.

"What we need now is the fourth book." Karas clambered up behind.

"How? How will all four help us more than three? You may have been searching for ten years, Karas, but I have more history with the books."

"With four books we could go back to the forest," Karas said.

Yes, there was that. But Johnis wasn't in the forest. He was here, in Alucard's talons.

"Of course, the fourth book. Just hurry."

JOHNIS AND MIRANDA STOOD OUTSIDE OF SALLY DRAKE'S house ten minutes later. The streets were empty except for one boy who leaned against the church, chewing on a piece of grass.

"Do you want to go in peacefully, or should I just go in, kill the tramp, and find the book on my own?"

"No need to cause a stir. Let me get the book."

"Remember: one false move and I will kill you where you stand."

He knocked on the door and waited for a few seconds.

A thin woman answered the door. "Hello?"

"Sally Drake?"

"Yes. May I help you?"

"My name is Johnis. I think you have something a friend of mine, Karas, left with you. A book. I would like the book."

She stared at him, speechless.

"Sally Drake?"

The woman blinked. "I . . . I'm sorry. For a moment there I thought you looked . . . Have we met?"

"Hurry it, please!" Miranda snapped.

Sally looked over Johnis's shoulder at Miranda. "I'm sorry, but I was told not to—"

Miranda flew past Johnis and slammed her gun against Sally's forehead. The woman dropped in a pile, unconscious.

Miranda stepped over the fallen form, muttering something about people not listening. Pulled Sally's prone body into the house.

"Get in here!"

Johnis stumbled in, dumbstruck.

"Find the book!"

She wouldn't let him out of her sight, which slowed their search some, but the house only had four rooms, including the kitchen. Miranda found the book in the larger of the two bed-rooms, under the mattress.

Black. Blood smeared on the first page. *The Story of History.*

Her eyes were fired with satisfaction. "Let's go."

"What about her? You can't just leave an innocent woman . . ."

"Innocent? She was holding one of the books, you fool! Karas is the one who's to blame for dragging her into this. Move!"

They left Paradise behind two minutes later. The sun was set-ting, time was fleeting, and Johnis was running out of options.

He had to make his play, and soon. The jet that would return them to Alucard's lair waited in a city to which they would fly in a smaller jet.

In the city, he decided. At the very least he would strike in the city.

twenty-one

"I s she okay?"

"Hurt but alive." Karas eased Silvie away from the house.

A police car with flashing lights sat in front of Sally Drake's home. They had already taken her to the hospital in Delta, twenty minutes away.

"And the book?"

"Gone."

"How do you know?"

"Because it's not where we agreed she would keep it. It's gone!" Karas yelled the last word, red faced.

"How long?"

"They came in a helicopter and were gone before anyone could talk to them. A man and a woman."

"Johnis! How long?"

"Ten minutes." Karas pressed her fingers against her temples. "This can't be happening."

"It *is* happening! They'll stop at nothing! How far could they have gone in ten minutes?"

"They were flying. They're gone."

A man dressed in a round hat and pointed boots eyed them from the sidewalk. Karas took Silvie's arm and led her across the street. The helicopter whirled in a field next to the church, ready for departure.

"We have to get out of here."

Silvie walked, numb, her mind buzzing with what they now must do. "We have to use the books."

"We only have three," Karas groaned. "We might as well have one. All we can do is enter the simulation—you know that. They're worthless!"

"Not to Alucard."

"What are you saying?"

Silvie angled for the helicopter and picked up her pace. "We have to trade the books for Johnis."

"Don't be stupid!"

Silvie whirled, furious despite the knowledge that Karas was being perfectly logical. "I'll tell you what was stupid!" She pointed a finger in Karas's face. "Going into Teeleh's lair to recover the first Book of History. Leading the Third into battle to rescue his mother. Betraying Thomas to save you from Witch! That was stupid!"

Karas's face lightened a shade.

Silvie continued, "Yet those were all things Johnis did, following his heart. Now he's in trouble, and you suggest I don't follow my heart?"

"That's not what I'm saying."

"Then what?"

"Follow your heart, but don't be stupid," Karas said. "You can't give Alucard all seven books! Your mission is to find them before the Dark One does, not to give the Dark One all seven to save your lover."

"You think I don't know the mission? I was chosen with Johnis. I was there when he went into the first lair. I was by his side when he risked his life to save you, or have you forgotten?"

"I don't see—"

"I'm saying that Johnis didn't follow perfect logic; he did what he believed was right in the face of terrible odds. And each time he ended up with a book."

"Then he was lucky."

"Luck had nothing to do with it. Johnis was chosen because he was willing to do what others were unwilling to do. It's in his heart! That is the *only* way to find the books."

It was the first time Silvie had actually thought of it in those terms, but saying it, she thought she might actually have struck on the heart of the matter.

"Think about it." She jabbed her head with a finger. "It's about the heart, not logic. The Great Romance, the fall from Elyon,

Teeleh's jealousy, the Horde, the lost books . . . all of these have to do with the heart. The only way to find the seven books is to follow your heart." She let out a long breath. "Johnis followed his. Now I will follow mine."

"But giving the books—"

"The right thing to do is to save Johnis, at all costs."

"Even if it costs the mission?"

"It's my mission to lose, not yours. Were you chosen?"

Karas looked at the helicopter, her jaw set. Silvie knew that she was wounding her friend, the only friend she had in this world at the moment. But she wasn't about to let the one man who'd repeatedly risked his life to save theirs be killed now. And yes, there was some self-serving messiness to this business. She loved Johnis. More than she loved the books, more than she loved herself.

"No," Karas said. "You were chosen. So I'll follow you. Like I followed Darsal."

"And did Darsal find the fourth book?"

"Yes."

"So then, have faith."

"Darsal also struck the deal with Alucard that put us in this mess."

Touché.

"As you say, I'm chosen. And I say we do whatever it takes to get Johnis back."

"Okay. We use the books to get Johnis back if we can. Any suggestions, chosen one?"

Silvie ignored the dig. "We get word to Miranda before she does anything foolish."

"And how do we do that?"

"The same way we got word to you. You need to get us on the Net."

"That could take some time, assuming anyone is even interested. You can't just walk up to a camera and spout off your personal messages for them to broadcast."

"Then we do something more inventive. Take someone important captive."

"Don't be ridiculous." She frowned. "You really want to do this, huh?"

"Every minute we talk takes him another minute farther from us. We have the only thing they need now. We use the books!"

Karas turned and walked toward the helicopter. "Here goes nothing."

twenty-two

He had to move, and he had to do it quickly. And judging by the switch they'd made from the helicopter to the small jet, moving on the ground was going to be more of a problem than he'd imagined.

Miranda had shackled him before landing, his wrists separated by a short length of chain, his ankles tethered together in the same way. Then, under the cover of darkness, she'd led him across the asphalt to the waiting jet. He was supposedly stronger than most in the Histories, but he was not strong enough to break the chains—he'd tried more than once and succeeded only in bruising his wrists.

"How high are we?"

She lifted her eyes. "High enough for you to contemplate your death for three or four minutes before being smashed like a bug."

"You think I would jump shackled like this?"

"I think you would save me the hassle of disposing of your body if you jumped without a parachute."

He frowned. There were some qualities about Miranda that he found appealing, he'd decided: Her obsession with the Books of History. Her ruthlessness in pursuing what she understood to be great gain. She would have made a good leader among the Forest Guard with the right heart.

"What do you really hope to gain in all of this?" he asked.

She grinned. "You have to ask? I stand in a room below the earth with Alucard. This beast who's lived for centuries and spawned only he knows what kind of evil upon this earth. Kings and their kingdoms have risen and fallen throughout history because of him."

He hadn't thought of it in those terms.

"He has more power and more wealth than any man who has ever lived. And yet he would trade it all for seven history books bound in leather. And you ask me what I hope to gain? The question is, what do *you* hope to gain?"

"I'm doing what was asked of me."

"Of course, how silly of me. These fuzzy white bats from your world."

"Elyon."

"The one who made this mess to begin with."

He turned from her and eyed the rear compartment door again. They would fly to Alucard's lair, and with nothing left to gain from his life, she would dispose of him.

A bell sounded, and Miranda snatched her phone to her ear. Listened.

He had to get the shackles off using the key in her pocket. But even now her eyes rested on him, watching, always ready. She had two of the guns, one in each of two holsters under her arms. One wrong move and he knew she wouldn't hesitate to kill him.

She suddenly stood, spun to the Net screen that hung from the ceiling, and pressed a button. The thin box blazed to life.

There, on a stage like the one they'd seen in the Rose Bowl, stood none other than Karas. The caption below her said they were at the Pepsi Center in Denver. A Tony Montana benefit concert.

Miranda muttered a bitter curse. "They have them! They took them from under our noses!"

Johnis stood from his seat. "The books?"

Miranda whirled. "Sit!"

He remained standing, his eyes on the Net, and she spun back, momentarily preoccupied. Karas stood center stage with Tony Montana to one side. Her voice suddenly filled the box.

"So listen up, people." She stepped to one side, and Silvie walked out to the microphone. In her hand she held a stack of three books: a black one, like the one they'd retrieved from Sally Drake's home; a purple one; a gold one.

She spoke in a shrill voice, yelling, staring right at the camera. "Alucard! Listen to me, you sick monster from hell! I have them." She held up the three books. "I have the last three Books of History."

She stopped, her eyes fiery and her breathing labored. Surely she realized that millions of people were watching this. It was why she was doing it.

But what, exactly, did she have in mind? Surely not . . .

"You want them? They're yours. Give me Johnis, and you can have them. That's all I ask. Give me the man that I love, and you can have these books and wreak all the terrible havoc you want."

"She's lost her mind." Miranda laughed. "She's gone completely mad. For love!"

"You know where I am. I'll give you until daybreak. If you don't come, I'm going to burn them!"

"She's really lost her marbles this time. Totally—"

Johnis seized her momentary distraction and rushed her then, covering the carpet between them in two strides, each at the limit of the chains around his ankles.

His fingers clawed at one of the guns under her arm before she could turn. He let his momentum carry him forward, and his shoulder slammed into her back with enough force to snap her spine.

She grunted and started to rise, but he didn't wait to see what damage he'd done. Her brown bag sat on her seat, and in that bag, the Book of History she'd taken from Sally Drake's home.

He snatched it up and dove for the rear compartment door. The sign above a yellow leather pouch read PARACHUTE. But he had no clue how to use it. Taking it, however tempting, would prove useless. He was a goner, but he'd already accepted that.

Unless . . .

He tried to shove the gun into his pocket, fumbled it, shoved harder, and managed to get it in. The book . . .

He glanced back and saw that Miranda was staggering to her feet, dazed but otherwise unharmed that he could see. Frantic and completely out of options, he thrust the book into his belt. Grabbed the lever he'd watched the charter pilot shut to seal the door.

Jerked it up. The door cracked, then flung wide. Wind tugged at him with a roar. He grabbed the parachute and glanced back at Miranda, who was lifting her gun.

Johnis threw himself into the wind.

MIRANDA STARED AT THE OPEN DOOR, REFUSING TO BELIEVE that Johnis had actually jumped.

The jet had lost some altitude but wasn't leveling.

He had the book. She'd watched him shove it into his jeans before throwing himself from the aircraft. How could anyone be so committed to any idea as to throw his life away for it? If he'd jumped for love, that would be one thing. But he'd jumped for one reason only: that she would not have all seven books. Nothing else made sense.

He was protecting his mission, Elyon.

Miranda blinked. She pulled the door to the cockpit open. "Note our position. Turn around and head back to Denver."

"Ma'am, that's a good hour back the way—"

"Now!" she screamed. "Turn back now!"

JOHNIS FELL THROUGH THE DARKNESS LIKE A ROCK.

The jet zoomed away at a rapid rate, a speck against the black sky now. Air howled past his ears, tugging at his shirt. He couldn't see the ground yet, so he gripped the book at his belt and tried see past the wind.

Three minutes she'd said. How anyone could be so high as to fall for three long minutes was beyond him, but his life now depended on it.

He fell for what seemed an eternity—looking, looking, and seeing nothing. And then that nothingness darkened, and he realized he was falling through a cloud. Closer to the ground then.

The idea that he could slam into hard earth at any moment sent his heart into another fit. He'd been falling for all of a minute or two, but it felt more like an hour.

He broke out of the clouds and saw the ground below, rushing toward him. So close already? This would never work! Never! At this speed he would be flattened like a bug splattering on the Chevy's glass.

The ground was there, just there, so close but still way too far away.

Johnis shoved his right forefinger into his mouth and bit deeply into his flesh. Warm blood wet his tongue—salty and alive. With his left hand he held the book in his belt tight and held his breath. He could see the trees now, the branches, the field beneath him, screaming for him.

Then, when he was sure he'd waited too long, he thrust his

bloody finger onto the book. The gateway into the skin-world gapped suddenly, a ring of shimmering air before him. He threw himself through it, squinting against the impending crash of earth against his body.

For a moment, pure silence.

And then . . . white.

Karas had told them about how the books had been separated from them when she and Darsal had used them to enter the simulation between the worlds. Johnis had to return *now*, while the book was still in his hand.

Before he was really anywhere, before he could fully arrive at the world between the worlds, Johnis lifted his finger from the book and shoved it back down.

The reversal into darkness happened before he could see any detail in the white world he'd been heading toward. He was back again, falling through the darkness after having jumped from the airplane. But as he'd hoped, his descent had been interrupted and now started over from a distance of less than a tree's height from the ground.

Johnis was so delighted at his success that for a split second he forgot that, although it might not be as destructive as falling from the clouds, falling from ten feet was dangerous enough.

The image of his leg bones slicing up through his belly flashed in his mind. Then the ground slammed into his feet, and his flying ended in a terrible crash. Johnis stood and tested his legs and arms. No breaks. Fantastic!

He looked around at a ring of trees, tall and dark, like claws reaching to the sky. His limbs were shaking, and his heart was pounding, but he'd thrown himself from a jet and lived to tell.

More importantly, he had the book.

It took him only a minute to shoot through his shackles using the gun, imitating the way Miranda had used it. An amazing weapon.

The chains still hung from his wrists and his legs, but he was free to move unrestricted. He had to get to civilization, find a phone, and call the number Karas had given him before Miranda reached them.

Hold on, Silvie. Hold on to the books; I'm coming.

Johnis ran into the night, fast, faster than seemed possible.

twenty-three

The Spartan Hotel was a veritable fortress that rose against the dark Denver skyline, a tower of glass and steel and, of course, lights. Lights were everywhere in this world.

Silvie paced in front of a window that filled an entire wall of the fortieth-floor suite Karas had whisked them away to after her announcement. The room overlooked Denver; it was an expansive suite with a separate bedroom on one side and a conference room on the other. Silvie and Karas stood in the lounge between the two, staring at the city lights.

"You're sure the message got through?"

"Trust me, if Alucard is alive, he got the message. And we know that Miranda heard of your little stunt in Las Vegas quickly enough. She's obviously on the Net. Your message was heard by the whole world, loud and clear."

"Then how long?"

"Even with our delays getting to the stadium, they couldn't have been more than an hour ahead of us."

"It's been an hour," Silvie muttered.

She flipped her bone-handled knife in her right hand for the comfort it brought her. They'd made it clear to a number of well-placed staff members at the concert that if anyone came looking for them or for the books, they would be in Karas's suite at the Spartan. Two guards from her team waited at each entrance, ready for any possible breach.

They had invited Miranda, but they wanted her to come on their terms, not her own.

"Just remember"—Karas glanced at the three books on the crystal coffee table—"no trade without Johnis."

"That's the whole point."

Karas humphed. "Don't think she won't try something."

"Which is why you have this place armed to the teeth. And we aren't exactly helpless." Silvie spun her knife into the air and caught it lightly in her palm.

"And if it's Alucard who comes?" Karas bit her fingernail. "I doubt we would be a match for him." And then she added as a muttered afterthought. "Not without a silver bullet, anyway."

"Bring him on!" Silvie snapped. "I'm sick of this whole business!" She tried to stem the tide of emotions that flooded her mind but failed miserably.

"Look at us! We started out with visions of slaughtering the

Horde to protect the forests, and that's simple enough, right? I could cut the heads off ten of the diseased Scabs and not suffer a single wound. I was Silvie! I could kill Horde! That's why I was chosen!"

She was yelling.

"But no, instead I followed Johnis into the desert and *became* a Scab!" Tears leaked down her cheek. "Instead of killing the Horde, I followed him into their city to *rescue* one! And then I followed him here, into hell itself. And he's lost." She struggled not to cry. "I'm lost, Karas."

"You love him." Karas came toward her.

"And does he love me?"

"Foolish question. Have you seen the way he looks at you?"

"But not enough to sacrifice his mission for me."

Karas stilled for a moment. "So that's it? You're angry because he seems to put this quest to save the world ahead of you?"

She didn't answer.

"You would sacrifice the mission for his sake, but you don't think he would do the same for you," Karas said. "Am I right?"

"Does it matter?"

"You said it yourself: he was chosen because of his loyalty to an idea. He doesn't distinguish his love for you from his loyalty to Elyon. To him they are one and the same."

She made sense, but it didn't ease Silvie's sadness, which she herself didn't understand. "You're right. I'm being childish."

"I doubt that's a bad thing in this situation. And I think Johnis loves you as much as he knows how to love. He's only sixteen,

Silvie. So are you. In this world people don't marry nearly so young. Give yourself time, for the sake of love!"

"Time." Silvie looked into the older girl's eyes. "Time is something the Horde never gave us."

Karas's walkie-talkie squawked. "We have an unidentified helicopter circling the roof. Just a heads-up."

JOHNIS HAD RUN THROUGH THE TREES FOR ONLY A SHORT time before stumbling upon the dirt road. And then he ran on the dirt road for about an hour before a house lit up the valley below.

He was hardly winded despite running at a full sprint for so long—at the moment this oddity was a small encouragement in the face of his predicament. But he seized it for what it was worth and ran harder. Faster. Perhaps twice the speed he could have mustered back in Middle.

He flew up the steps that led to the farmhouse, twisted the handle, and shoved the door hard without bothering to knock.

With a splinter of wood the door swung open and Johnis stood in the frame, facing a family of four seated around a table, sharing a meal.

They stared back with round eyes. The father dove for the kitchen, and judging by the scowl on his face, he wasn't running away. There was a weapon in his sight.

Johnis threw up both hands. "No harm! I just need a phone. Please, I'm no enemy!"

The man of the house swung into view, holding a long gun in his arms. Johnis's second encounter with a shotgun since coming into the Histories.

"Don't shoot!"

"Elvis!" The wife stood. "Don't you dare pull that trigger!"

The two seated boys gawked at him. "Shoot 'im, Dad!" the smaller said.

"You broke our door," Elvis said. "I have every right to shoot you where you stand."

"And I wouldn't blame you. But the truth is, I only need to make a call, and then I'll leave. Please, it's urgent."

"What's so urgent?"

"I'm lost."

"No, you ain't. Not no more."

"Please, please, I beg you. If I don't make the call, the world as you know it could be in terrible trouble!"

They stared in silence, considering his words.

"Shoot him, Dad," the older child said.

"Don't you dare," the wife snapped. "For heaven's sake, let him make his call."

"YOU'RE RIGHT," SILVIE SAID, TAKING A DEEP BREATH. STILL no sign of any approach except for the helicopter, which hadn't been reported again. "I'm just a bit emotional."

Karas offered a comforting smile. "You're doing much better

than I did. Then again, I was a ten-year-old brat dumped into Las Vegas. You should try that . . ."

A thump sounded down the hall, cutting her off. They both turned toward the door. The cell phone Karas had set down on the coffee table vibrated, loud in the sudden silence. Silvie picked it up and handed it to Karas.

"Answer it," Karas said softly, stepping toward the door.

Silvie flipped the thin black wafer open and pressed it to her ear, the way she'd seen Karas do a hundred times since their meeting. "Yes?"

Johnis's voice filled her ear. She froze. "Johnis?"

"Silvie! Thank Elyon, Silvie. You're safe?"

"I . . . oh, dear Elyon, thank you." She was trembling. "Are you okay? Yes, I'm safe, of course, I'm safe. Where are you?"

"Listen to me, Silvie. Just listen carefully. Miranda is on her way. You can't give her the books. I have one. I have Karas's book. Do you hear me? Do not give up the three books."

So he was safe then!

"I hear you. I—"

"There's more. Alucard has the other three in Romania. He's been here for over two thousand years, waiting for us. And Miranda . . . I think she may have been infected by him. I hit her with enough force to break her back. You hear what I'm saying? She's not any ordinary woman."

"Johnis, I—"

The door suddenly crashed open in front of Karas. Miranda stood in the opening, gun leveled, lips twisted.

"Not one move." Her eyes flashed to Silvie. "Drop the phone, honey."

"She's here! At the Spartan—"

The gun spit a bullet at her. She jerked and felt it slit the air by her left ear.

Miranda dove like a cat attacking a mouse. She twisted as she passed Karas, striking her jaw with her heel. Karas staggered backward, stunned by the sudden assault.

And Miranda, this woman Johnis claimed had been infected by Alucard, was already halfway to Silvie, with her gun extended.

Silvie's instincts kicked in. She threw herself back and to the right, knowing the coffee table with the three books rested there, just behind her.

She felt her body flip into the air and complete a full loop, flying farther than she'd anticipated before slamming into the window.

Two bullets punched holes in the window.

"Do you really want a fight, lover girl?" Miranda crouched between Karas and Silvie. "Because, believe me, I can. I will."

She plucked the phone from the carpet and spoke into it. "Good-bye, Johnis." The device shattered in her hand.

Silvie stood.

"You may have brought a few tricks from this other world of

yours, but I have it on excellent authority that you can't stop bullets. My aim is much better if I want it to be."

Silvie looked at Karas for direction.

"How did you get past my men?" Karas asked.

"I'll assume that was a rhetorical question." Miranda whipped out two sets of shackles and tossed one to each of them. "If you think Johnis is out of the woods yet, you don't know me well. We track every step he makes. Put the cuffs on, and I promise you'll see him again. Refuse and I'll be forced to kill you now. So sad."

Silvie blinked. She had no doubt that Miranda could and would do precisely what she said.

"We don't have all night. The helicopter is waiting."

twenty-four

"Silvie? Silvie! Silvie, for the sake of Elyon, answer me!" Johnis screamed the last, unable to stem the fear that raged through his mind.

He could hear the miserable witch in the background. *Do you really want to fight, lover girl?*

"Fight her, Silvie! Kill her!"

Miranda answered. "Good-bye, Johnis."

Click.

He pulled the phone back and stared at it. Then yelled into it again. "Silvie? Silvie!"

The family of four stared at him. He slammed the phone on the counter and paced a quick circle, hands kneading his face, mumbling, "This can't be, this can't be, this can't be . . ."

"Easy, man," the farmer said. "You're not making sense."

The small one gained the courage to voice his curiosity. "Who's Alucard?"

Johnis spun to the father. "Do you have a jet?"

"A jet? No."

"I have to get to Romania, man. You have to help me get to Romania! There's a castle up in the mountains, with a dungeon. Worms larger than a grown man, a Shataiki. Alucard. He has Silvie . . ."

They just looked at him, dumbfounded. A candidate for the fruit farm. How could they understand a word he was saying with their limited knowledge?

"Then how about Denver? You've heard of the Spartan?"

"The hotel? Denver's a good two hundred miles—"

"And I need to get there. It is absolutely imperative that I get there before that witch leaves."

Miranda was probably already gone, but there was a chance that Silvie and Karas had evaded capture. Or managed to hide the three books before Miranda could get her paws on them.

"You're nuts."

"Do you have a Chevy?"

"I have a Ford truck, but if you think—"

"I'll buy it." Johnis withdrew two coins and tossed them in one palm so they clinked loudly. "These are gold. I'm told gold is very rare here. You could buy two Chevys with this gold. I'll buy your Ford, and you drive me to Denver."

The man eyed the coins skeptically. "How do I know they're real? You don't drive?"

"I do. Most excellently. But that's my offer. I buy, you drive."

THE JOURNEY TO DENVER IN THE TRUCK WAS A HAIR-RAISING affair, because Ted Blitzer insisted on "learning you how to drive proper," as he put it. The road was rough, and the car bounced like a frantic mare, wearing a blister in Johnis's right palm. He found himself yearning for a Chevy. At the very least, a good stallion.

Ted jabbered like a monkey, but Johnis's mind was on Silvie. And the books. And Alucard. And the Roush ordering him into the Black Forest to meet Teeleh. Honestly, he had difficulty remembering exactly how he'd come to this place, bucking down the road in a Ford truck, listening to Farmer Ted talk about how the government was conspiring to steal all the land from rightful owners.

A war is brewing, Ted insisted. He couldn't know how little any war meant compared to what would happen if seven ancient, leather-bound books got in the wrong hands. It could all be over in just a few hours now. In a day or two the whole world would know just how critical the words they'd heard Silvie speak from the stage at Tony Montana's concert really were.

They'd all seen her hold up three books and cry out her challenge to Alucard. The earth hung in the balance of those three books, the three in Alucard's lair, and the one inside his belt.

The farmer took over when they neared the city, and Johnis

stared ahead, pretending to listen. But his mind was gone, and his hands were sweaty, and his heart was breaking for Silvie.

Ted dropped him off in front of a towering glass building with huge red letters that spelled out SPARTAN HOTEL and left to find his brother.

The moment Johnis stepped past the double glass doors, his worst fears were confirmed. The main atrium was closed off with yellow tape, behind which a dozen police officers worked over several bodies on rolling beds.

"Silvie?" He leaped over the tape and sprinted to the first body. A white sheet covered the victim's head. "Silvie?"

He ripped off the sheet. A man.

"Hey!"

He bounded to the second body, discovered it was another male.

"Hey! Hey, you can't do that!"

As was the third victim.

He whirled to the approaching office. "Where's Silvie? And Karas?"

"Out!" The officer jabbed his flashlight at the door. "This is a crime scene, buddy."

"Please, I need to know if Karas . . . Kara Longford is one of the victims."

"Out!"

Another policeman stepped in from his right, grabbed Johnis by his arm, and escorted him past the yellow tape.

"Please," he whispered, begging. "Just tell me if there were any women among the victims. I have to know."

"Are you a relative?"

"To whom? One of the victims? How would I know unless you told me who they are?"

"Speak to OIC." The officer shoved him past the door and pulled it firmly shut behind him.

Johnis turned around, saw that several officers were watching from beyond the glass, and faced the street. He stood on the sidewalk, immobilized by indecision.

He was one among a sea of onlookers in a huge city of blazing lights, and he was alone. Lost. A dozen alternatives screamed through his mind.

He could hijack a Chevy and try to find the jet field. Foolish.

He could take an officer captive and force them to take him to Romania. Absurd.

He could stand atop the police car parked in front of him and begin to scream at the top of his lungs. Hold up the one book in his possession. Hope that the cameras would put him on the Net so that Alucard could come after him . . .

But he couldn't risk giving up the book now, not even for Silvie's sake. Could he? Alucard now had six of the books. The one in Johnis's belt was the only thing that stood between the Shataiki and—

Johnis caught his breath. The riddle in the desert pool exploded in his mind.

Beyond the blue another world is opened.
Enter if you dare.
In the west, the Dark One seeks seven
To destroy the world.

The west was this world, he knew that now—paradise gone amuck. But how would the Dark One destroy this world? By doing what the legends said he'd done once before. Release the Shataiki from the desert reality into this one. What if the seven books could create a breach between the worlds, allowing the Shataiki to physically swarm into this world, destroying it as they had after breaching the barrier between the Black Forest and the Colored Forest?

What if evil showed itself in physical form in this world as it had in his world? The sea of humanity in front of him became Horde? This was something for which Alucard would patiently wait two thousand years.

He withdrew the black book tucked in his belt. Turned it in his hands. Fanned through its blank pages. According to Karas, the *original* seven blank Books of History didn't work like the rest of the blank books.

One of the original books could take you to a simulation called Paradise.

Four books could take you from one world to the other.

All seven books could undo the rules that governed these books and create a breach for the Shataiki. Maybe worse.

Tears of desperation filled his eyes. *I'm sorry, Silvie. I don't know what to do.*

"Johnis."

He spun to his right. A woman stood on the sidewalk, her arms by her sides, heels together. She wore jeans and black boots. A red blouse hung on her thin frame. Her hair was long and dark next to skin so pale that it seemed to glow in the night.

All of this Johnis saw in a blink. But it was the scar on her cheek that his eyes settled on. His heart jumped.

"Darsal?"

Her eyes scanned the street as she hurried to his side. "Come with me."

"What . . . how's this . . . I thought—"

"You thought what they think. That I'm dead." She took his arm and guided him down the sidewalk, glancing around nervously. "Do I look dead to you?"

"What . . . what happened?"

She spoke in a rush, quickening her steps. "I just flew in from Turkey, where I've had my head buried in the caves for two weeks. And what do I see? A news story of Silvie, standing on a stage, holding up three Books of History. I got here as soon as I could."

Darsal looked at him. "You look like you've seen a ghost."

"We all thought you were dead."

"Karas made herself known. I made myself dead. They have the three books?"

"How long . . . ?"

"Ten years, just like Karas. Where are Silvie and the books?"

"But Alucard had your book!"

Darsal stopped. "You . . . you've seen him?"

"They took me."

"Miranda. To Romania." She walked again, practically dragging him now. "I had to let them have the book to complete the illusion that I was dead. I'd arranged for a doctor to confirm it, take my body, but the book left no doubt. One book by itself was no use to me anyway." She paused. "Where is Silvie?"

"They have her."

Again Darsal stopped. Fear spread through her eyes. "And the books?"

Johnis took a breath and looked at the book in his hands. It shook slightly. "Six of them."

Her eyes dropped to his hands. Then back up to his face.

She spun and began to run. "Hurry!"

Johnis gripped the book tight and ran after her. "Where?"

"They'll be coming! We can't let them have that book!"

He sprinted after her, around a corner into an alley. And then she began to run, really run, like the wind.

As did he, feeling a surge of confidence with each step.

They flew by an old drunk, who must have wondered what had been slipped into his drink. She came to a puddle and took to the air, leaping twenty feet, with Johnis in the air behind. They landed lightly and sprinted on without missing a step.

Darsal's car waited on a corner a mile from the Spartan. She vaulted over the roof, threw the door open wide, and spun in. Clearly she'd had plenty of experience.

Johnis slid in beside her and slammed his door. "It's a Chevy?"

"As a matter of fact"—she jerked the car into gear and it surged forward—"yes."

Johnis looked at her. "A good choice."

"You're the expert?"

"Granted, I'm useless in most things here, but I know a thing or two about Chevys."

"It's a bit disorienting at first. I found some clips from your episode in Vegas. You've done just fine." Darsal forced a smile.

The last ten years had made her a hard woman, he could see. Elyon only knew how she'd managed on her own for so long.

"Billos—"

"I don't want to talk about Billos," she snapped. "Only one thing matters now."

"Silvie," he said. "They have Silvie and Karas."

"The books," Darsal said. "First we lock your book so deep in a vault that no one finds it. *Ever,* if need be."

"And then?"

She stared ahead and blew out some air. "Then we go after your girlfriend."

twenty-five

T he night air smelled of Shataiki. It was all Silvie knew for certain.

Miranda had chained their wrists and ankles, taped their mouths with gray cloth, and pulled seamless black hoods over their heads before summarily dumping them into a jet's cargo compartment.

She could hear Karas's breathing beside her, locked in darkness. And as the jet screamed down the strip and angled for the sky, her last hopes of Johnis coming to their rescue fell like a rock.

All was lost. Silvie allowed herself silent tears. Her ploy had failed miserably. She replayed the events in her mind over and over and concluded that their mistake had been in underestimating Miranda. Who could have guessed that she would have been able to overpower so many guards and catch them with the books without having to trade Johnis? Johnis's warning had come too late.

His voice echoed in her head. *I hit her with enough force to break her back. She's infected.*

Infected by Alucard? This is what gave her the strength to overcome the guards. Their only hope, however slim, now rested in the other words he'd spoken into her ear. *I have one. I have one, Silvie.*

He had a book. But one book was no advantage against Alucard.

The flight had lasted hours—how many, Silvie could not estimate. She only knew that the air was cool and quiet, which led her to believe it was night, when hands had jerked her to her feet and had pushed her from the aircraft.

They'd traveled up twisty roads for an hour and finally came to a stop—still night, as far as she could tell. Still not a word from Miranda, or anyone, for that matter. They were hustled through cool, damp air into what she guessed was a stone chamber or hall. She could tell because of the faint echo that came with each breath Karas took.

A door thumped shut behind them. Still no word.

They were led by chains down the hall into a stairwell. Down, down, feeling their way along the stone walls on either side. And she knew when the first scents of Shataiki reached past the hood that they'd entered Alucard's lair.

The floor flattened, and they slogged over wet ground. Beside her, Karas protested with a muffled cry. The odor of sulfur was strong enough to make one blanch—unlike Silvie and Johnis, Karas had been away from the Shataiki scent for ten years.

A soft popping sounded high overhead. Worms nestling in their own gook. Silvie swallowed. A hand tugged on her chain. She stopped. For several long seconds they just stood there. She could hear a flame crackling, could smell the smoke mixed with the scent of rotten eggs. Heard the worms she imagined overhead.

The sound of someone breathing. Nails clicking on the stone floor.

"Take them into the main chamber." Alucard. Silvie's blood froze in her veins. The voice was low and breathy, backed by a growl that reached into the pit of her stomach.

They were led deeper, down another flight of stone steps, wetter and slipperier than the previous one. She could hear the same squealing they'd heard below the monastery in Paradise. Worms in torment, far away.

Her desperation deepened with each step she took. They must be a hundred feet below the earth's surface now. Maybe twice that. Even if Johnis did find a way to the castle, there was no way he could save them.

She'd loved him. She'd kissed him, and she'd known with that kiss that she would marry him. If she died in the next ten minutes, she would cling to that memory, that single moment of comfort between them.

I love you, Johnis. I love you.

She slid, caught herself on a rail, then eased her foot to the next step. Her chain tugged.

I love you, Johnis. I love you.

The cry from the tormented worms grew at an alarming rate. And with the clunk of a latch and the protest of rusty hinges opening, the squealing became a scream, directly overhead.

Silvie gasped under the tape. Again someone pulled her forward.

They entered the room of screaming worms; she could smell them, hear them, feel their slime underfoot, taste their foul odor. It was a vast room, judging by the echoes off the stone walls.

A hand stopped her. The chamber fell to silence.

It occurred to her that she was panting through her nostrils. Dizzy from the hyperventilation, she tried to calm herself.

"Move," a gruff voice commanded. Hands shoved her.

She stumbled forward, tripped over a ledge, and fell headlong onto a three-foot-high riser. Karas grunted beside her. They were hoisted to their feet and clamped into brackets on the wall.

The hoods were ripped from their heads, tape from their mouths. A hooded guard with large red lumps on his face turned and walked away from them.

Silvie gazed at the chamber near the guard's torch as he slumped toward the large black door through which they had entered.

The room was perhaps one hundred feet per side. Dozens of columns bridged the span from the wet floor to the ceiling. The worms nested there: gargantuan worms that looked like white logs twisting slowly in their own mess. Thousands of them, interwoven in a blanket that looked twenty feet thicker on one end than on the other.

A sizable table engraved on all sides with Teeleh's winged serpent image sat squarely in front of the wall adjacent to them.

Larger worms clung to three of the walls, including the wall they were chained to, but the wall facing the single ornate table was free of not only worms but also their mucus. Dry stone ran from floor to ceiling. And on this wall . . .

Silvie blinked. She'd seen this. These concentric circles. Exactly like the circles on the covers of the seven Books of History.

"It's a gateway," Karas said. "They've built some kind of a gateway!"

The door slammed shut, pitching them into darkness once again.

She could hear the worms writhing in wetness. The thought that one or more might slide over them made her shiver. She tugged at her chains and was rewarded with nothing more than a rattle to break the stillness.

"Are you okay?" Karas asked.

"No. Honestly, I think I might be dead."

Silence.

"You heard him," Karas said.

Another shiver went through Silvie. "It's him."

"Alucard."

"He doesn't have all seven books," Silvie said.

"He's going to use them to open a gateway," Karas replied,

casting no confidence behind the notion that Alucard wouldn't soon have the seven if he didn't already.

"You can't know that."

"Don't you see?" Karas was whispering with urgency now. "The Books of History are a gateway to truth, to understanding, to knowledge, to history! They connect what can't be seen with what can be seen. The other world with this world—we experienced that ourselves."

"That doesn't mean he's going to use the books to connect the two worlds," Silvie said, though she wasn't so confident.

"Why else would Teeleh send him here? What can he do here that he can't do there? Teeleh intends to wipe out Earth with a virus that makes the Raison Strain virus look like a common cold."

"With Shataiki," Silvie said. "He invaded the Colored Forest exactly as the legends say. Now he will invade this world."

"With Shataiki."

twenty-six

Whatever Darsal has done during the ten years since the books deposited her in this world, it has brought her wealth and resourses that might be as extensive as Karas's, Johnis thought.

She'd whisked him to the airport, where a jet waited, fueled and whining on the runway. They would make one stop in a city called New York, where she kept one of her homes; then they would cross the Atlantic for Romania.

Stopping to secure the sole book in their possession would cost them an hour, but Darsal was unwilling to risk putting all seven books in the same country, particularly Romania.

Johnis agreed. They were only two or three hours behind Miranda, if their calculations were right. Securing the book would put them into Bucharest four hours after Silvie, assuming Alucard had taken her to the same mansion he'd taken Johnis to.

"Which he has," Darsal said, spitting to one side on the runway as they boarded the jet. Alucard had done many things in his time, but none of it compared to what he intended to do now in that unholy place.

The jet flew at twice the speed of sound, faster when it climbed out of the atmosphere. This meant little to Johnis, as long as the book was safe and they reached Silvie while she was still alive.

"Tell me, Darsal," Johnis said. "Tell me everything."

She sat across from him in a black leather chair, legs and arms crossed. Her eyes diverted to the night sky over the Atlantic. "I can't."

There was enough emotion in those two words to strike fear into Johnis's heart. "You can't? Why not?"

"Because not everything can be spoken of easily, Johnis!" she snapped. "You've spent a month or two of your life frolicking about on this grand adventure. Try ten years and see if you can survive!"

She pressed her fingers together to cover her nose. Closed her eyes. "I'm sorry; that wasn't called for."

"Well . . ." *Well what, Johnis? You have no clue what horrors Darsal has suffered these past ten years.* "We've all paid a price."

She was about twenty-seven years old now, he realized. But ten years without the harsh sun had been kind to her face. Her hair was very dark next to her pale cheeks. Something about her had changed, but he couldn't put his finger on it. Her nose, perhaps? No, it was that she'd lost weight.

Karas had been a child in the other world and had grown up here without the benefit of fighting the Horde. Darsal had been a well-muscled warrior, who'd thinned out in a world without constant battle. In some ways, she was more beautiful than he remembered.

But life here had hardened her in other ways.

He wanted to ask her about Billos. About what she knew of Alucard. The books. Karas. All of it. But Darsal looked distraught, tapped out, nearly ruined.

So Johnis told her about their own journey, starting back in the forest, chasing her and Billos into the desert. Finding the Black Forest. Landing outside Las Vegas. Stealing the Chevy.

Instead of grinning at their antics, Darsal unsuccessfully fought back tears, managing only a smile or two when he described how he'd mastered the Chevy.

He told it all, hoping to remind her of home. To reconnect. And then he sat still, letting her process.

"I have something I have to tell you," she said softly, refusing to look Johnis in the eye.

"Then tell me."

"I can't. Not yet. It's too terrible."

"Will it affect our mission?"

Darsal sighed. "Is there nothing but the mission for you?"

"Yes! There's Silvie. There's getting back to Middle! There's life, because if we fail, I have a feeling there won't be any."

"Fair enough." She paused. "When I arrived in Las Vegas, I

was as lost as you. Karas was a young child then, and I had no way of contacting her. By the time I learned that the entertainment mogul was actually our Karas, I had already made the connection with Paradise and tracked the books back to Turkey and then from Turkey to Romania, where I learned that Alucard had been sowing his disease. I got too close to him and exposed myself. It was then that I decided that he and Miranda, that witch he'd taken up with, had to think I was dead."

"Sounds dangerous."

"Dangerous? Is there anything about this mission that hasn't been dangerous? I managed to pull it off—amazing what a pile of money and the right medical clinic can do for you these days."

"So what do you know about Alucard?"

"I know he plans on opening a gateway for the Shataiki. I've been in the chamber where he keeps his worms."

"The library," Johnis said.

"You've been in his dungeon?"

He told her.

"Then you know where we're going. The gateway chamber is deeper than the library you were in. That's where he'll do his deed. And that, my friend, is where we're going."

She stopped then, as if she'd come to the end of it.

"That's what you needed to tell me?" Johnis asked.

Darsal set her jaw. "This is all a bit much. We'll have time later." She reclined her seat and closed her eyes. "Get some sleep. We're going to need it."

THE NIGHT WAS STILL BLACK WHEN THEY PULLED THE CAR off the road and ran through the woods, around Alucard's mansion an hour north of Bucharest, Romania. They could see two cars parked at the front, a good indication that Miranda had brought them here, as suspected.

They both ran with silver guns firmly fixed to their hips and two long knives on each thigh. Dressed in black from head to foot, Darsal carried a few supplies in a pack at her belly, but other than that, they were going in lean.

They'd made the change on final approach into Bucharest. Darsal had given Johnis lessons on aiming and firing the guns, and she assured him that after fighting the Horde, it was child's play. Just point and shoot, and brace for a slight kick.

The stone mansion stood dark against a starry sky in the center of the clearing they faced. Asleep by all exterior indications. No lights, no smoke from chimneys, no guards, no sounds but the nearby chirping of crickets.

"Follow closely!" she whispered, breaking from the tree line.

Darsal ran in a crouch, ahead and to his right. They flew through the grass like crows from above. Crossed the hundred yards of cleared ground in a matter of seconds.

They stopped with their backs to the rear wall, listening. Nothing.

Darsal pointed to a stone well they'd passed twenty feet away. "We're going down."

"Into the well?"

But she was going already.

Darsal slipped like a cat over the lip of the well, gripped a rope hung at the center, and disappeared into the earth.

A quick tug convinced Johnis the rope would hold them both. He swung out into the well and lowered himself after her.

Down. A hundred feet. Into utter darkness.

It occurred to him that there was no scent of water. A dry well then?

"Here!" Her hands tugged at his shirt and stopped his descent. She pulled him into a tunnel built into the wall. "Water was drawn here when the well was operational. Stay close."

They hurried through the darkness, using their hands to guide them along the wall. He could hear her breathing, the sound of her boots padding on the rock. But he still could see nothing.

She stopped and put her hand on his shoulder. "Okay?"

"Okay."

"There's only one way to do this, and it won't be fun. A ventilation shaft runs down to the right just ahead. It leads to the gateway chamber. There aren't any gates to stop us."

She said it as if this alone weren't good news. "But?"

"But there are worms." She pulled something from her pack and handed it to him. "It's a raincoat with a hood. You're going to need it."

They slipped into the plastic suits, and she pulled him forward. "The more speed you hit them with, the easier it will be to get through. You don't want to get stuck in the middle. Trust me."

So. This is why she'd been coy about the details of their rescue attempt. They were going to try to slide through a nest of worms. The thought made him shudder.

He smelled the terrible scent of rotten eggs before he felt the hole open on his right. Slime on the walls confirmed they'd reached the air vent in question.

"You've done this?"

"More than once. Go on your back, feet first." She engaged her gun with a loud clank. "Go down with one gun ready."

She was serious.

But even she was hesitating. "Remember, the faster the better."

"Hold on. What can we expect past the worms?"

"A ten-foot drop into the chamber. The gateway. With any luck, Silvie."

Then she threw herself into the shaft and slid away, like a log down the mud waterfalls south of Middle.

Johnis withdrew one of his guns, chambered a round as she'd shown him, held the weapon close to his chest, pulled the hood over his head, and jumped into the slimy tube.

The worm gel was even more slippery than he'd expected. He slid down the chute like a rock, eyes clenched, breath held against the stench. Then his boots slammed into a soft body, and he was in the nest.

Squeals of protest filled his ears. He was all the way in, from head to foot, and he could feel the soft, lumpy bodies on his cheeks. And he still wasn't through!

Panicked, he gasped. A mistake. The taste of the worm gel was no less offensive than its odor. And then he was out of them, falling free. He opened his eyes for orientation, but it was dark, and gel was thick over his face.

He landed hard, rolled once, and came to his knees, the breath knocked clean out of him. The goo . . . he had to get the goo out of his eyes. The gun in his fist prevented a clean swipe of his face, but he managed to get most of the stuff off.

Johnis jumped to his feet, his gun extended in the dark.

Fire hissed loudly five feet from him, and he saw that Darsal had ignited a flare from her pack. Her hood was back, and she'd managed to avoid getting any of the mucus on her face.

Johnis glanced around the room, saw no immediate danger, and shrugged out of his plastic suit, glad to be dry. His stomach was on the verge of protesting violently, but he held it in check. Free now, he could think straight.

And see the worms on the ceiling. The huge concentric circles on one wall looked exactly like the rings on the books' covers.

"Johnis?"

He spun to the sound of Silvie's voice. She stood against the far wall next to Karas—shackled.

Johnis reached her in four long bounds, dropped his gun at her feet, and fumbled frantically with her cuffs. But the metal clasps were locked tight.

"Easy!" Darsal whispered.

"Darsal," Karas said. "I thought . . ."

"Do I look dead?"

"What . . . what happened?"

"Later. Right now we have our hands full."

"Thank Elyon," Silvie breathed. "Thank Elyon!"

Johnis grabbed her face and kissed her. She returned the kiss, and not till he pulled back did he think about the worm salve on his skin. She didn't seem to mind.

"Don't thank him too quickly." Darsal glanced about the room. "We have to destroy the gateway and get out alive."

Silvie and Karas were shackled along a wall that contained chains and metal clasps for four people. Miranda or Alucard had the keys, and the steel links were an inch thick.

"How do we get them out?"

"Not with a bullet, if that's what you're thinking. Too thick. We'll have to figure out how to get the key."

"What?" Karas cried. "Are you crazy? We have to get out of here!"

"No, we have to destroy the gateway."

"He doesn't need a gateway! He needs the books. This is all symbolic."

"Yes and no. He needs a place to gather the Shataiki that come through. He also needs a nest for the females. With Shataiki, males lay worms that females fertilize." She crossed to the wall and lit a torch. Yellow flames lapped hungrily at the air.

"A typical flame won't do much to this stuff, but get enough heat and their mucus will go up like gasoline."

"Well, then," Johnis said, "we have our way of destroying them."

"Problem is, we're in here too. Along with the books."

"Then what do you suggest?"

Darsal walked closer to them, eyeing the large black table that stood before the concentric circles formed on the wall. "I don't know. Part of me thinks we should just burn the books with this stink hole. From everything I've seen, they are as evil as Alucard."

What was she saying? Johnis glanced at Silvie.

"You can't do that," Karas said.

"Can't I?" Darsal eyed her, wearing a crooked smile. "I think I've earned the right to do whatever I need to do. The books killed Billos, didn't they?"

"You know he's dead?"

"He was left in a dungeon filled with Shataiki!" Venom laced her voice. "Of course he's dead! Either that or he's Shataiki himself." She forced a smile. "All hail the books. We should probably burn every last one."

The change in her took Johnis off guard. After ten years, she held on to a bitterness that could not be easily dismissed.

"But first we have to figure out how to get out of here." She turned her attention to the gateway. "I've been in here three times, and each time I can't help but think that there's something about the circles that look wrong. Do you see it, Silvie?"

Johnis stood by her side and looked at the gateway. The stone rings looked like they'd been melted in rather than placed. Nothing else that he could see.

"We can't stand here discussing the gateway!" Karas snapped. "Miranda could step in now, and we'd be finished."

Darsal walked closer to Silvie. Jumped up on the ledge, eyes on the rings. "At the top of the rings, the worms avoid contact."

Silvie and Johnis glanced up.

Darsal moved in that moment, when both of their eyes were diverted. She shoved Johnis's hand back and slammed a shackle over his wrist before he knew what she was doing.

It locked on contact.

Johnis moved without thought. He snatched up the gun with his free hand and spun to Darsal, who'd stepped off the ledge.

"What are you doing?" Silvie cried. "Have you lost your mind?"

"Yes, Silvie." She lifted her hands and gave Johnis a condescending smile. "I have lost my mind. I lost it with Billos in Alucard's dungeon ten years ago."

"Don't think I won't use this." Johnis kept the gun trained on her.

"Would you, Johnis? Would you really shoot one of the chosen ones? Go ahead, pull the trigger."

He lifted the barrel to the ceiling and pulled the trigger.

Click.

"You don't think I'd be foolish enough to give you a loaded gun, do you? After what you did to that Chevy?"

"What's the meaning of this?" Karas snapped. "You think that witch Miranda won't kill you as quickly as she kills us?"

"No, I don't think she will."

"Why not?"

"Because I am Miranda."

What? She was speaking figuratively, Johnis thought. He'd seen them both within the last twenty-four hours, and apart from their hair and their height, their frames, their eyes . . . He stopped.

"This isn't Middle, my friends. This is 2033. Masks and cosmetics have come a long way."

They stared at her, grappling with the notion that the woman they'd known as Miranda had actually been Darsal all along.

"Why?" Karas cried.

Darsal drilled her with a dark stare. "Maybe you'll understand before it's all over. Which only gives you a few minutes."

A door to their right suddenly swung open. The large Shataiki named Alucard stood in its frame, staring at them with yellowed eyes. For a long moment no one moved. No one seemed to breathe.

"Do you have it?" the beast said.

Darsal, who was Miranda, reached into her pack. Withdrew the seventh book. The black one that Karas had hidden and that Darsal had made a show of securing in New York. Her deception had run as deep as her bitterness.

She walked up to Alucard, who stepped into the room.

"The seventh book, sir."

twenty-seven

Flames crackled from seven lampstands that Miranda had lit around the table in front of the gateway. A thin trail of oily smoke rose from each, spreading before reaching the nest of worms writhing above. With each passing moment, their agitation seemed to increase, as though they, too, had waited an eternity for this moment.

On the table stood two finely crafted wooden candelabras holding seven colored candles, each which Darsal now lit. A silver bowl filled with water sat to one side.

All of this made sense to Silvie. Symbols from Other Earth. Colored candles on wood symbolized the Colored Forests from the legends. Water symbolized Elyon's water. But two other objects on the end of the table were less obvious to her. A framework that looked somewhat like the drowning gallows that the Horde used, and two crossed planks.

At the center, lit clearly by the wavering flame, lay the seven Books of History, side by side. The black one Michal had first given them on the left. Then the brown, the blue, the green, the purple, the golden, and another black.

Alucard stood across the room, watching Darsal quickly prepare the table. He turned with her wherever she went, as if he feared turning his back to her for even one moment. It was the way evil worked, Silvie thought. Distrusting.

So this was it? All they'd fought for came down to this moment, far below the earth, in the Romanian mountains? The search for the six missing Books of History, the love that had blossomed between Silvie and Johnis, the . . .

She swallowed at the lump gathered in her throat. "Why haven't they killed us?" she whispered.

"They're going to drown us." Karas's eyes glistened with tears. "Either that or crucify us. It's how he does it."

"You can't know that," Johnis said. "He's gloating after two thousand years of waiting; he's relishing—"

"Silence!" Alucard thundered.

The beast glared at them with yellow eyes. His mangy black coat looked like it hadn't been groomed once in the two thousand years since he'd vanished from his lair in the Black Forest— a few days ago for Silvie and Johnis, ten years for Karas and Darsal.

"How could you do this?" Johnis's voice cut through the room, heavy with bitterness. He was speaking to Darsal. "How could you betray Elyon?"

A roar crackled through the air; Alucard's wings spread wide, his jaws tilted to the ceiling. Rather than feeling any fear at his display of rage, Silvie felt some consolation in the fact that he still reacted so strongly to the name of their maker.

"And who betrayed Billos?" Darsal snapped, ignoring both Alucard's order for silence and his roar.

"You!" Johnis cried. "You're betraying him right now!"

Darsal faced him, her expression drawn and red. "Who made a mockery of the Great Romance by stealing the one love I've known for the sake of these cursed books?"

"You. You're making a mockery of the mission."

"Shut up!" she screamed. But she couldn't hold back. "If it weren't for these books, none of us would be here!" She stepped closer, jabbing the air to accentuate each point. "There would be no Shataiki or Horde. I would have died for Billos! Do you understand that? He was my life!"

"And you blame Elyon? Don't be a fool!"

"I made a vow, and Elyon help me, I'll keep it or die with Billos!"

"What can you hope to achieve by this?"

A crooked grin split her face. "You know what I hope to gain. These larvae need a female to complete their transformation into lovely black butterflies with fangs. The worms in this hall are female. Once they've been fertilized, there's no turning back."

"We begin!" Alucard snarled. He walked toward the table, and with each step his claws clacked on the stone floor.

"Please, Darsal." Johnis could beg all he liked—she didn't look interested in bending her decision to betray Elyon, Silvie thought. Embittered by her loss of the one man she was willing to die for, Darsal had sworn to wage war on the books and whoever stood in her path to do so.

"We begin!" Alucard growled again.

Darsal's fierce glare drilled Johnis for another long beat. She turned her back to them and walked to the table under Alucard's watchful gaze.

Why was the beast so attentive to her? Clearly there was some bad blood between them.

"Why him?" Karas whispered in a voice so faint that Silvie could barely hear her words. "Why is she cooperating?"

Karas's eyes were wide, and her face glistened with sweat. The thin white blouse she'd worn was now badly smudged and wet. She looked at Silvie.

"If she's waging war . . ."

"Don't, Darsal," Johnis pleaded. "You can't open the gate! They'll only destroy you."

No reaction this time.

Alucard stood over the seven books like a hawk over a nest of chicks. Saliva dribbled from pink lips and pooled on the table. Darsal stood to one side, eyes on the beast, jaw firm.

Alucard reached for a long knife, held his paw over the silver bowl with water, and slashed himself.

Blood dripped into the water.

Johnis put his free hand in Silvie's and held tight, perhaps to still the tremble in his own fingers. "He's defiling the water with blood," he whispered, citing the taboo they all knew. Silvie didn't know if the rite Alucard was performing was necessary to open the gate, but she suspected it was more a matter of mood setting for the beast after two thousand years of dreaming.

He flung the knife to one side, letting it clatter off the table and fall noisily to the floor. Facing him, Darsal picked up the black book and set it on the table directly in front of him.

The beast squeezed blood from his wound onto the cover, then pulled his claw back.

Darsal set the brown book squarely on top of the bloody black book. Now there were two books, one atop the other, joined with blood.

Again, Alucard dribbled blood onto the cover.

This was the vision that they'd seen beneath the waters at the desert oasis. All seven books aligning to create a gateway.

"Darsal . . ." Johnis didn't bother imploring this time. Just "Darsal," and it was clearly for his own remorse. *Darsal, Darsal, what have you done?*

One by one Darsal set the books on the stack as Alucard wet their covers with his blood until there was only the second black book left to set on top.

Instead of placing the book on top, Darsal held the book out to him. "This one should be yours to place, sir."

Alucard hesitated. Clearly this was not as rehearsed.

He took the book, uttering a soft growl. Held it over the sixth book with both hands. Lifted his head to the stone gateway before him.

He spoke in a low, crackling voice that filled the room. "By the power entrusted in me, for Teeleh, my master, and his precious blood, which gives life to all who despise Elyon and his waters, I call you forth . . . my bride."

Darsal eased to one side of the table, her eyes on the books.

Alucard lowered the last black book.

A flash of light cracked above the books. Silvie threw herself as low as her chains would allow her. Above them the worms began to squeal.

"Elyon, help us," Johnis breathed, gripping her hand even tighter.

The light slammed into the stone wall and ran a ring around the perimeters of the concentric circles. Alucard spread his wings, lifted his jaw, and roared, "My bride!"

The gate dissolved into light, humming with the power of a thousand lightning bolts. Silvie couldn't breathe. Her heart felt as though it had been crammed into her throat.

The first streak of black that cut through the light was a Shataiki guard, the kind that had flocked above Silvie and Johnis in the Black Forest. Roughly two and half feet of shrieking muscle, with large yellow fangs.

And then they came in a dizzying rush, dozens in the space of a few seconds, flying to the ceiling, where they hooked their claws into the squealing worms and hung, glaring with red eyes.

It's over, Silvie thought. *We've lost.*

But then everything changed.

Darsal moved. The smaller Shataiki were still flying through the breech, and Alucard was still glorying over his coming bride, and Darsal was moving like lightning.

She grabbed one of the wooden candlesticks and flung off the candles, rounding the table in long strides. The candlestick was now a long, sharpened stake.

Screaming at the top of her lungs, Darsal thrust the wooden stake under Alucard's raised arm. Into his heart.

An earsplitting crack from the beast's throat shook the chamber. A single, oversized Shataiki spilled out of the light and landed on the ground beyond Alucard. The female had joined her guard. And more of her guard flooded the gate.

Alucard spun about, slashing at empty air. Skin fell from his face, exposing bleached bone.

Darsal leaped over the books, snatched up the second candlestick, and descended on the still-disoriented female.

"I knew it!" Johnis cried. "I knew it!"

She sidestepped a thrust of Alucard's claw, dove for the female, and plunged the second stake into the creature's chest.

Silvie watched in disbelief as both Alucard and the female who would bring his offspring to life began to melt before them. Their flesh fell from their bodies like rotten flesh falling from an over-ripe fruit. Unable to hold their own weight, they fell to the ground, writhing.

Dying.

Darsal stood back, eyeing them. Silvie knew then that Darsal, chosen alongside Silvie and Johnis and Billos, had planned this all along.

Still the Shataiki flooded the chamber.

twenty-eight

I knew it!" Johnis said. "The key, the key, hurry!"

Darsal stared at him.

"Darsal . . ."

What was she doing? She'd saved them, right? She'd planned this whole thing down to the final touches: winning Alucard's trust by giving him her book, pretending to be filled with bitterness, knowing that one day the others would come through and Alucard would have the advantage. He would beat them to the books. But she would be there to kill him, having learned precisely how to kill Shataiki in this reality.

Everything else had been lies. She'd lied to them so that Alucard wouldn't have any reason to doubt her. And she'd turned on him only when he was at his weakest, in the moment of his own glory.

She'd done it.

Hadn't she?

"Darsal," Johnis breathed. "Please, no, no, no! Tell us that you've stayed true!"

Darsal spit on Alucard, who was now a shivering blob. She crossed to the table and stood before the seven Books of Histories.

For a moment she just stood there, her back to the others.

Stop it! Silvie thought. *Break the connection. Shut the gateway!*

Instead, Darsal spun around, thrust both arms into the air, and screamed at the bats still swarming into the chamber.

"It's her!" Karas cried. "Darsal is the Dark One!"

So then not everything Darsal had said had been a lie. She'd intended on killing Alucard all along, but she was as bitter as she'd let on.

Darsal screamed at the ceiling, full throated, veins pronounced on her neck and arms. But now tears ran down her face. She took one long draw of air and screamed again, until Silvie thought she might tear her throat.

"Elyon!" Johnis wept. "Elyon compels you, Darsal. Elyon compels us all."

"No!" Darsal whirled to Johnis. "Elyon made the Dark One, you fool! Don't you see? I am the Dark One. The prophesy was about me! I am destined to destroy this world. I've turned my back on Elyon!"

She was right.

"I haven't turned my back on Elyon." Johnis's eyes darted to the

Shataiki filling the room. A thousand it seemed. For a moment Silvie thought she saw some white fur among them, but then it was gone.

"You may be the Dark One, but you can't deny Elyon's power," Johnis said. "Or his will to take the diseased and bathe them in his water!"

Darsal was breathing hard, her eyes fiery, desperate. But she had nothing to say.

"It doesn't matter why you did what you did any longer!" Johnis cried. "It only matters what you do right now."

Her face wrinkled. Shataiki streamed in over her head. On the ground, Alucard and his bride convulsed, then stopped moving.

The worms stopped squealing. Except for the steady beating of wings through the gateway, the room fell silent.

The Shataiki suddenly began to fall to the floor, chunks of rotting fur raining from the ceiling by the hundreds. They thudded on the stone and immediately bowed their heads to Darsal. The ground was quickly carpeted with black bats except for a large circle around Darsal and the two dead Shataiki.

Silvie blinked. Having lost one master, they were acknowledging another: Darsal.

The Dark One.

"Is Elyon so foolish?" Johnis demanded.

Darsal was out of words. Now it was tears that came from her in streams, wetting her cheeks.

"Do you think he allowed you to become this so-called Dark One without knowing it would work to his advantage?"

What was he saying?

"He knew that in this moment you would do something not even you have anticipated. That was why he chose you! He knew you would stand against evil! You will undo all that Alucard has done by saving the books."

She shook her head. "No . . ."

"You, this Dark One, will embrace Elyon's love, that same love you felt for Billos, and you will destroy evil."

"No . . ."

"Because you are not evil. Evil has just consumed you. But they . . ." Johnis pointed at the hundreds of Shataiki now on the ground, bowing to Darsal, tempting her with their service. "They are evil!"

"Nooooooo!" Darsal screamed, weeping. "Noooooo!"

"Yes!" Johnis cried. "Yes!"

Johnis began to weep. Darsal sank to her knees.

"End it, Darsal," Johnis said. "You've killed Alucard. Now rid yourself of his evil."

She let her hands go limp by her sides, sobbing, her face tilted up, eyes closed. "I'm the Dark One," she mouthed. "I'm the Dark One."

"Fight, Darsal! Fight for Elyon." Then in a raw voice that made Silvie want to cry, "You are the chosen one!"

It was as if this truth had hit Johnis for the first time. Darsal might have convinced herself that she was the Dark One, but even being the Dark One, she was the chosen one.

Silvie suddenly felt the weight of the idea and began to cry with them. Because she, too, was the Dark One, wasn't she? They all were, as much as they were all Forest Dwellers, without Elyon's cleansing waters.

Yet they were chosen. It was up to them to follow either the one who had made them dark, or the one who had chosen each of them.

Teeleh or Elyon.

"No, no, no, no, no, no . . ." Darsal was rocking, sobbing the words.

Shataiki continued to stream into the room.

"Please, Darsal," Karas cried. "Please . . ."

Without warning, another larger Shataiki spilled through the gateway, landed next to Alucard's dead body, and flapped to steady itself.

"Darsal!" Silvie screamed.

She jerked her head up at the warning, seeing the second female. She stood shakily, staring, gathering her wits.

And then something behind her eyes snapped into place. She rushed the dead slab of meat that used to be Alucard and jerked the stake from its heart.

Screamed, red-faced.

Rushed the second female from behind.

Slammed the stake into its back, right through the rib cage, through whatever innards filled the heartless creature, and right out its chest.

She held the stake in place, resisting the attempts of the flailing beast to break free.

"Back to hell!" Darsal thundered. Then again, in a voice that cracked with emotion, "Back to hell!"

She released the stake and staggered back, breathing hard. Her heel struck her bag, and she stopped. Still Shataiki poured in through the gateway.

"Darsal . . ."

It was all Johnis needed to say. Darsal's face wrinkled with anguish for just a moment. She glanced up, saw the beasts bowing to her, and swept up her bag. Flung it sidearmed at Johnis.

"The keys!" Silvie cried. "Quick!"

Johnis frantically rummaged through the bag.

Darsal was already sprinting toward the Books of History, scattering the Shataiki gathered there. She grabbed the stack of books with both hands and tore the top three from the table with a grunt.

The light vanished immediately with a crack that echoed through the chamber. The upper halves of two Shataiki spun from the closed gateway into the room and fell to the floor, dead lumps of bleeding fur.

Darsal's sudden change of heart wasn't lost on the thousands of Shataiki gathered on the floor. They began to bob and shriek with open jaws, like begging chicks in a nest.

"Hurry!" Darsal grabbed the other four books and sprinted for them.

Johnis found the keys, freed Silvie, and was working on Karas.

Thoughts of servitude no longer in their minds, the Shataiki began to take flight around the room. First a dozen, then a hundred, then a thousand, shrieking and flapping in a river of black just below the worms.

Darsal kept one eye on the Shataiki and one on the bag as she withdrew first one, then two flares.

The bats gained courage and began to sweep down, snapping their jaws. Above them, the worms were screaming.

Darsal shoved a flare at Silvie. "Light it by ripping the cap off. It's hot enough to ignite the worms' mucus. This place will go up like a tin of gasoline."

Johnis had freed Karas, and now himself.

"Run!" Darsal jumped off the ledge and streaked for the shut door. Silvie followed hard after her. A bat brushed through her hair, and she cried out, swatting at her head.

"Light it!" Darsal slammed open the latch.

Silvie slid to a stop. She jerked the cap off the flare. It hissed and spouted red flame.

The Shataiki grew frantic. They flew every which way now, shrieking, crashing into the walls, clawing at the stone.

"Light it!" Darsal screamed again, throwing the door open.

Silvie thrust the flare against the worm salve on the wall. It sizzled but refused to light.

Shataiki had found the open door and flew out above Darsal's head now, dozens, shrieking as they disappeared.

"Go, go, go!"

Karas ran out, followed by Johnis.

Darsal snatched the flare from Silvie. "Go!"

"You—"

"Go!"

She went. Through the door.

A plume of orange flame and heat mushroomed behind her, and she spun to see Darsal tearing for the door.

The flame spread along the walls like ignited oil on water. *Whoosh!* Silvie stood like wood, stunned by how rapidly the fire consumed the room.

Shataiki, now totally aware of their impending demise, clogged the door. Behind them a huge ball of fire fell screaming from the ceiling. A burning worm.

"Go, go, go!"

Darsal tugged her. Slammed the door shut. Bats thudded into the wood. Even outside, the roaring flames were deafening.

Then they were running up the passage. Silvie was the last up the stairway into Alucard's library, where more worms crowded the ceiling. Darsal had ripped open her flare and was lighting fire to one of the wet walls behind the bookcases.

"Get out!"

No Shataiki, Silvie saw. They'd already flown out.

They waited for Darsal by the door this time, until her flame caught. The library went up like a tinderbox, chasing them out the door with heat and flames.

Darsal led them from the fortress in a full sprint. Out into the cool night air. Just in time to see a black stain winging frantically for the sky.

Shataiki screeched overhead, scattering to find safety.

Silvie spun back to the castle. Light flickered from the hallway past the door. And when she stilled her breath to listen with the others, she could hear the distant cries of burning Shataiki and igniting worms.

Alucard's lair was being consumed by hell.

twenty-nine

Johnis, Silvie, Karas, and Darsal stood on the side of the road for a long time, watching and listening to the flames. Little was said. Much was considered.

Silvie looked up at the graying eastern sky. "Morning is coming."

And for a while, nothing more was spoken.

"We did it." Johnis looked at the seven Books of History that Darsal had placed on the ground. "We have finally found the seven books."

For a few long beats they all just stared at them. Darsal's shoulders shook with a sob. She hugged herself with one arm and lifted the other hand to cover her face.

"No, Darsal." Silvie put her arm over the girl's shoulder. "You can't blame yourself."

"I . . . I . . ."

"You are chosen," Johnis said. "And you saved us all. That's all that matters now."

It was hard to imagine what kind of suffering Darsal's bitterness had caused her all these years. *She will bear that scar,* Silvie thought. But Johnis was right. They had won. They were the chosen ones, and they had recovered the seven books.

"There's still danger. The books can still be used." Karas picked up the black one and wiped Alucard's blood off its cover using a tissue from her pocket. "What now?"

"Now we have to return them," Johnis said.

A whoosh of wings disturbed the air behind Silvie, and she spun around, expecting Shataiki. But this wasn't a wad of black muscle.

It was a ball of white fur: Roush. Michal!

And hard on Michal's heels, Gabil landed a ways off, tumbled three full turns on the ground, and launched himself into a spindly but much improved karate kick.

"Hiyah!" he cried, and then landed on both feet where he managed to keep his balance. "What do you think? Was that better?"

Silvie now realized that the white streak she had seen among the flood of black Shataiki had been Michal and Gabil! They stood like two soldiers on the grass, green eyes glimmering, fur so white they looked like the marshmallows Karas had served them with coffee.

Karas rushed up to Gabil and dropped to one knee. "Thank Elyon!" She hugged the Roush. "How is Hunter?"

Gabil nearly toppled backward with her hug. "Easy, easy! My improved skills don't include protection against the hug of death! Hunter who?"

"The Roush who guards Middle?"

"Oh, *Hunter*," Gabil said. "As full of himself as always, I'm sure."

Johnis hurried up to Michal, dropped down to one knee, and bowed his head. "You have no idea how good it is to see you, Michal."

A thin grin crossed the Roush's lips. "Actually, I do."

Then they all crowded around the two furry, white bats, peppering them with questions and offering details about their close call with Alucard. And in short order, some things were finally set straight.

Yes, both realities were linked in so many ways that not even Michal had known before. Thomas of Hunter's dreams were indeed true, all of them, in both places. Teeleh's attempt to destroy the world through the disease borne in Shataiki—the Horde disease—was now foiled.

But in reality, Thomas of Hunter's greatest tests remained ahead of him. He might be a figure of history here in the Histories, but he was still the leader of the Forest Dwellers in a war that was being waged against the Horde. And things were about to get very nasty.

"Then we have to get back!" Johnis paced a tight circle. "Now!"

"You can if you wish," Michal said. "But five years will have passed when you arrive there."

"What? How's that possible?"

"I've been forbidden from allowing you to influence events there now that you know what you do."

"But five years! What's happened in five years?"

"The world has changed. You'll see."

Silvie put her hand on Johnis's arm. "How old will we be? There, I mean?"

Gabil flashed a grin. "Old enough to be blissfully married, if you so choose; no worries there, Silvie. And if you like, I could perform some of my—"

"Please, Gabil," Michal cut in. "No one wants to see you stumble through your karate moves at a wedding. Get a grip on reality, will you?"

"No." Johnis looked at Silvie and winked. "We would love to see Gabil perform at our wedding, wouldn't we, Silvie?"

She felt so buoyed by his statement that she nearly threw her arms around his neck and kissed him in front of them all.

"Yes." She returned his wink. "Yes, we would."

Michal nodded. "So I take it that you two would like to go back with the books?"

"If it's okay," Johnis said.

"Of course."

"When?"

"Now. But five years will have passed."

It was a heady idea, Silvie thought.

"Does it matter if we stay or return?" Karas eyed Darsal.

"Of course it matters. But it is your decision entirely. Wherever you live, you will have challenges, as long as evil remains unbound."

"And what about the Shataiki?" Darsal glanced above her at the gray sky.

"Yes, them. A few dozen escaped, wouldn't you say?"

"Maybe more. But they were males."

"And there are no females." Michal shrugged. "I would worry more about the others."

Karas looked up. "Others?"

A worried look crossed Darsal's face. "You're saying the rumors are true?"

"There's usually at least some truth in a rumor."

"What are you talking about?" Karas demanded.

"The vampires," Darsal said. "Alucard's been a busy beast all of these years."

Silvie listened with interest, but the greater part of her mind was on the forests. The faster she could return, be it five years or five hundred years from now, the better.

Darsal nudged a stone with her foot. "I have to know something."

"Whether or not you were the Dark One," Michal said.

Her eyes met his.

"Johnis was right," the Roush said. "You are both fallen and chosen. As are all of you. And your choices aren't finished. Do you follow?"

"Billos . . ."

"Gone. To save you. But you knew that."

She nodded gently.

"I'm proud of you, Darsal. After falling so hard, you stood. But please, try not to fall again."

She smiled.

"So it was all about this . . . these books?" Karas asked. "Paradise, the worms, the monastery. Thomas Hunter."

"Yes. And no. Yes, the lost books are now found, and this chapter is over. But as I said, Thomas has only begun to face his challenges in the forests. And here . . ." Michal glanced at the nearby forest. "Here it's all about the sinner."

The Roush said it with such a mix of passion and frustration that Silvie cringed to think what could ruffle such a stoic creature as Michal.

"Now, what will it be? Who's going, who's staying?"

Karas stepped up to Silvie and hugged her tight. "This reality is my home now. I have a world that needs some saving."

She sniffed and hugged Johnis, then Darsal.

"This place holds too many terrible memories for me," Darsal said. She was forgiven and she'd saved the day, but she was still wrestling with all of it. "I don't know what I'm going to do back in the forests without Billos, but I can't stay here."

"Then you'll be coming with us," Johnis assured her with a

slight grin. "We'll find a way to put what we now know to use, I'm sure."

Darsal offered a weak smile. "That's what concerns me."

They looked at each other in silence for a moment.

"There you have it, then." Michal waddled to where the books lay on the grass. "The books have been recovered, the quest is finished, the mission has been successful. The end."

And so it was.

Or was it?

the end

THE BOOKS OF

CIRCLE TRILOGY

CIRCLE GRAPHIC NOVELS

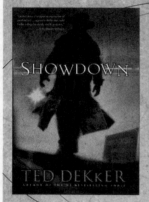
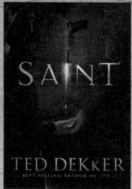

AN EXCERPT FROM

TED DEKKER'S NEXT NOVEL . . .

ϨINNER

COMING SEPTEMBER 2008

CHAPTER ZERO

MARSUVEES BLACK reread the words penned on the yellow sheet of paper, intrigued by the knowledge contained in them. He felt exposed, almost naked against this sheet of pulp that had come his way.

August 21, 2033

Dear Johnny –

If you're reading this letter, then my attempt to help you has failed and I've gone to meet my Maker. I don't have much time so I will be brief. None of what's happened to you has been by accident, Johnny—I've always known this, but never with as much clarity as now, after being approached by a woman named Karas who spoke of the Books of Histories with more understanding than I can express here.
Where to start . . .

The world is rushing to the brink of an abyss destined to swallow it whole. Conflict between the United States, Israel and Iran is escalating at a frightening pace. Europe's repressing our economy. Famine is over-running Russia, China's rattling its sabers, South America is battling the clobbering disease—all terrible issues, and I could go on.

But these challenges pale in comparison to the damage that pervasive agnosticism will cause us. The disparaging of ultimate truth is a disease worse by far than the Raison Strain.

Listen to me carefully, Johnny. I now believe that all of this was foreseen. That the Books of Histories came into our world for this day.

As you know, the world changed thirteen years ago when Project Showdown was shut down. Myself and a dozen trusted priests sequestered thirty-six orphans in the monastery in an attempt to raise children who were pure in heart, worthy of the ancient books hidden in the dungeons beneath the monastery. The Books of Histories, which came to us from another reality, contained the power to make words flesh. Whatever was written on their blank pages became flesh. If the world only knew what was happening!

Billy used the books to write raw evil into existence in the form of Marsuvees Black. A living, breathing man who now walks this earth, personifying Lucifer himself. He (and I cringe at calling Black anything so humane as a "he") was defeated once, but he hasn't rested since that day. There are others like him, you know that by now. At least four maybe many more, written by Black himself from several pages he managed to escape with. I believe he's used up the pages but he's set into motion something that he believes will undo his defeat. Something far more ominous than killers who come to steal and destroy in the dead of night. An insidious evil that walks by day, shaking our hands and offering a comforting smile before ripping our hearts out.

Billy may have repented, but his childish indiscretions will plague the world yet, as much as Adam's indiscretion has plagued the world since the garden.

Yet all of this was foreseen! In fact, I am convinced that all of these events may have been allowed as part of a larger plan. The Books of Histories may have spawned raw evil in the form of Black, but those same books also brought forward truth. And with that truth, your gifting. Your power!

And Billy's power. And Darcy's power. (Though they may not know yet)

Do you hear me, son? The West may be overrun with a populace that teeters on the brink of disbelief while at the very same time being infested with the very object of their disbelief. With incarnate evil! Black and the other walking dead.

But there are three who stand in the way. Johnny, Billy, Darcy.

Black is determined to obtain the books again. If he does, God help us all. Even if he fails, he escaped Paradise with a few pages and can wreak enough havoc to plunge the world into darkness. I am convinced that only the three of you stand in his way.

Find Billy. Find Darcy. Stop Black.

And pray, Johnny. Pray for your own soul. Pray for the soul of our world.

David Abraham

Marsuvees frowned. *Yes, pray, Johnny. Pray, for your pathetic, wretched soul.*

He crushed the letter in his gloved hand, shoved it into the bucket of gasoline by his side, and ignited the thing on fire using a lighter he'd withdrawn from his pocket after the first reading. Flames whooshed high, enveloping his hand along with the paper.

He could have lit the fire another way, of course, but he'd learned a number of things from his experimentation these last years. How to blend in. Be human. Humans didn't start fires by snapping their fingers.

He'd learned that subtlety could be a far more effective weapon than some of the more blatant methods they tried.

Black dropped the flaming page to the earth and flipped his wrist to extinguish the flame roaring about his hand. He ground the smoldering ash into the dirt with a black, silver-tipped boot and inhaled long through his nostrils.

So, the old man had known a thing or two before dying, enough to unnerve a less informed man than Black. He already knew Johnny and company were the only living souls who stood a chance of slowing him down.

But he was taking care of that. Had taken care of that.

Marsuvees spit into the black ash at his feet. Johnny's receipt of this letter would have changed nothing. It was too late for change now.

And in the end there was faith, hope and love.

No . . . in the end there was Johnny, Billy, and Darcy. And the greatest of these was . . .

. . . as clueless as a brick.

HAVE YOU JOINED THE CIRCLE?

SEE VIDEOS, READ TED'S BLOG,
FIND OUT ABOUT NEW BOOKS &
SIGN UP FOR TED'S NEWSLETTER AT

TEDDEKKER.COM

TED DEKKER is known for novels that combine adrenaline-laced stories with unexpected plot twists, unforgettable characters, and incredible confrontations between good and evil. Ted lives in Austin with his wife LeeAnn and their four children.